DOUBLE

Best wishes
Hetty Waite

DOUBLE
X

HETTY WAITE

Matador
Unit E2 Airfield Business Park,
Harrison Road, Market Harborough,
Leicestershire. LE16 7UL
Tel: 0116 2792299
Email: books@troubador.co.uk
Web: www.troubador.co.uk/matador
Twitter: @matadorbooks

ISBN 978 1803135 335

British Library Cataloguing in Publication Data.
A catalogue record for this book is available from the British Library.

Printed and bound in Great Britain by 4edge Limited
Typeset in 11pt Minion Pro by Troubador Publishing Ltd, Leicester, UK

Matador is an imprint of Troubador Publishing Ltd

To my mum, without whose support this book would never have been completed.

Email recovered from the computer of Ava DeLavier, Prime Minister of Great Britain in the year of the Epidemic, March 2061:

Commander Valance,

I fear it may be time to utilise the army to gain control of the streets of London. This disease has shown itself to be resilient and multi-layered. So far, the majority of my cabinet are either seriously ill, isolating at home in fear for their lives, or dead. Also, if my scientists are correct, we are not yet at the peak of this viral plague.

It seems that the virus attacks only the Y chromosome, causing most, if not all victims, severe pain before they are completely incapacitated. Death follows swiftly.

The result of this is a gender divide: men (with the XY chromosome) are dying, while women (with the XX chromosome) are seemingly immune, apart from mild symptoms. As you can imagine, this is building a climate of bitterness, hatred and fear. A rebel group of men, calling themselves the Ys, are leading assaults against the government, calling for protection to help them survive in these unprecedented times.

In addition, there are rumours of an even more distressing turn of events. Stories about creatures attacking the people of the city are becoming commonplace. Tales of beasts with red eyes and the skin of lizards are leading to mass hysteria. Shops have been looted. Violence against Ys is growing. It seems more and more likely that this Epidemic is evolving to cause mutations rather than simply death. If this is the case, then God help us all.

I understand how stretched your resources are and realise that as this disease spreads far and wide, many of your soldiers will be affected. I can only hope this missive reaches you in time to plead for help. We need armed forces in the City as a matter of urgency.

I desperately await your response and can only hope that I have reached you in time.

Good luck and stay safe,

Ava DeLavier

PROLOGUE

The street looks clear. Seemingly empty. Only a child is visible, a toddler really. She reaches grubby hands into an open bin, looks hungrily for scraps. A bruised peach is grabbed; she gnaws greedily on it, juice squirting onto her already sticky face.

A rustling begins, originating from behind a stash of burnt-out refuse containers. The noise grows into a strangled cry, but still the girl is oblivious. It is not until a figure emerges from its hiding place that she understands the danger.

A Y staggers towards her, knees dropping to the ground, hands scrabbling madly at his clothes. His face twists and convulses, like a circus clown pulling faces in the hall of mirrors.

Next, a terrifying sight. Something bursts from his skin, unzipping his human body as if taking off a jacket. This thing … it rips through the flesh and pulls itself free. Stretching up to its full height, the beast towers over the tiny girl: seven feet of scaly, reptilian skin. Jagged teeth glisten with venom that drips patiently to the pavement as the creature eyes her. With metallic claws glinting, it approaches, dropping onto all fours to advance, letting out a piercing screech as it makes its move.

BANG!

A loud crack rings out. In an instant the creature's head explodes, covering the girl in thick crimson blood and bluish-green goo. A woman stands behind her, holding a shotgun, breathing heavily. An older girl hides in her shadow. Grabbing the younger child's hand, the woman pulls her close:

"Cara, NEVER leave my side in these streets again. And never, EVER, turn your back on a Y."

CARA

ONE

One of my earliest memories is the first time I witnessed a Y transformation.

I must have been about three years old. We were moving between city hostels at the time, trying to find safe havens. There weren't many back then. Ys were still running free without controls, so the risk of them becoming infected and mutating was high. The army was struggling to keep control: so many soldiers had died, they hardly had any manpower left, and the ones they did have were at risk of changing. It's a shame that, at the time, the army was overwhelmingly made up of Ys.

Why I was out alone in the street at that age is anyone's guess. Myla always says I must have been on the hunt for food, as I never stopped eating. We'd joke about poor parenting skills leading to kids being made breakfast by monsters.

At the time I didn't laugh, though. I can still remember how hard my heart pounded, how afraid I was, when this human-lizard hybrid looked at me like I was human-shaped snack. I can still remember my Mum's angry, hysterical shriek as she yelled at me. I can still remember Myla peeking out from behind her legs, barely six years old herself, shaking in fear as she witnessed her mother killing a Saurian to save her little sister.

Unfortunately, that's no longer the worst monster I've seen.

*

Now

"Things haven't always been like this," Myla explained solemnly, staring each of the young girls in front of her straight in the eye. My sister always had liked the sound of her own voice, so presiding over a hall full of people meant she was totally in her element. Her audience looked suitably enthralled, so she continued, standing up and placing one booted foot on the bench.

"If you can believe it, the Ys once ran things. Society was known as a patriarch*ee.*"

Myla extended the final syllable to show her distaste for this ridiculous-sounding world order. Even though each recruit had sat through this history lesson many times, they all laughed and shook their heads as if this information was completely new to them. I was impressed – they had already worked out that they needed to keep Myla on side if they were going to get anywhere in this city.

"Yep, the Ys had the best jobs, earned more money and had most of the power. There were always calls for us Xs to be treated the same, equality and all that, but it never really happened. The Ys just loved the control. They weren't called Ys then, of course. Men. That was how they were referred to. And Xs were women. Like we were lesser than them." She smirked, her brown eyes flashing menacingly over the Y slaves standing silently at the side of the room. They carefully avoided her gaze.

"Of course, the Epidemic sorted out the strong from the weak – it came down to science. Those with Y chromosomes proved more vulnerable than those with the double X. The Xs rose to power, and that's where we've been ever since."

She sat back down and folded her arms, looking smugly around her. A sea of faces looked up at her, pale speckles standing out from the dark mahogany-lined hall.

"Can you remember it, this patriarch*ee*?" questioned Tyra, one of the new recruits. Big mistake, I thought. Without meaning to, she was challenging Myla's knowledge.

"Of course not, this was 13 years ago! I was only about five and Cara was a toddler!" She glanced at me for the first time, rolling her eyes conspiratorially before re-fixing Tyra with a withering stare. The young girl blushed and studied her feet furiously.

I cleared my throat. "It's all the battles you've been through, Myla, they must have aged you. Plus, you are the ultimate authority on the past. The founders of Galex passed on their memories to you, so we'd never forget how the world used to be." I knew my sister well enough to know that a bit of flattery could always be relied on to dampen her temper. Tyra shot me a grateful glance.

"Well, anyway," Myla continued, slightly mollified and

clearly unwilling to give up the centre stage, "things are different now. I took over two years ago, and our military power has gone from strength to strength." She drained the large, chipped mug she was drinking from, before holding it up and clicking at the nearest Y. He hurried desperately to keep her drink topped up to avoid giving her an excuse to punish him. Not that she always needed an excuse. Myla had been known to beat a Y so violently he never walked again, for something as simple as holding her stare, or for tripping and spilling a plate of food on the floor.

"But the might of Galex isn't just down to me and my stellar leadership!" Again, she flashed me a grin that didn't quite meet her eyes, her shiny dark ponytail swishing as she moved her head. "My sister, Cara, in her role as City Protector, has done an excellent job of training up a first-class army, who are destined to take on the Saurians and defeat them once and for all. It seems the scientists still can't find a definitive way to weaken them or a vaccine to stop the transformations, so it's up to us soldiers to find a different way forward. We have the city: next step, the world!"

The thirty or so girls around cheered, with some even chanting Myla's name. Many stood up from the benches they'd been sitting on to clap, eyes shining with excitement. Myla lapped up the attention, feet now crossed one over the other, resting on the table. I studied her: her eyes had that hard, steely edge that told me trouble was ahead. I could usually help rein in her wilder, more savage tendencies, but I was afraid: when she uncovered my secret, I knew it would change our relationship forever. It might even cost me my life.

*

Then

As children, Myla and I did everything together, despite being opposites in a lot of respects. She was dark, I'm fair; her eyes brown and mine green. Personality wise, it was the same. Myla was outgoing, cunning and wild. I was quieter, more cautious. These differences didn't matter though: we were sisters, we had a bond. She was fiercely protective of me, calling me 'Little Sis' from about as early as she could talk. I couldn't envision a world without her.

I was born a year or so before the Epidemic took hold in the early 2060s – a powerful, highly infectious virus which attacked anyone with a Y chromosome – namely, men.

They became violently ill. We're talking blood being vomited everywhere. Agonising pain, which left them writhing on the ground. And, inevitably, death. If they were lucky.

Because that's not the end of the story – you're probably thinking, okay, so all the Ys died out and the Xs were left to start again. Cue happy ending for girl power. Nope. Not that simple. Not all of the Ys died. Some simply … mutated.

Imagine. About half the people you know could transform into a monster at any time. Your parent could become one. Your brother. Uncle. Boyfriend. And it could happen anywhere: at home, at work, in the street.

Suddenly, nowhere seemed safe. Your property could be invaded; the rules of society no longer applied. Chaos descended and the priority became survival, at any cost.

The world got scary really quickly. We were lucky: our mum tried to keep us safe when all hell was breaking loose around us. I think it's why Myla is the way she is: she had to learn to be incredibly tough at a young age, to protect us. I know something happened with our dad; something neither she nor Mum would ever tell me about. Growing up in this world, it changes you. It leaves invisible scars.

Well, that's what I tell myself anyway, when I need to justify her actions to my conscience.

*

Now

"The final part of tonight's ceremony is to present each new warrior with their armour," Myla announced, after demanding quiet by banging her cup on the wooden table. A hush had descended as the girls finished their meals and rose to their feet in a line, preparing to accept their reward for months of hard training.

"Each and every one of you has proven yourself to be strong. To be brave. To be ruthless. You have earned your place in the Galex army, and you will be part of our future ambition to rid the world of the Saurian threat."

Myla pushed back her long brown hair to reveal her own metallic chest plate.

"I earned this fighting on the front line. Risking my neck when the great push took place."

Callie and Becka, the closest recruits to me, looked across inquisitively.

"She means when we expelled the last of the Saurians to beyond the city walls," I whispered.

"Oh, of course," breathed Becka, her blue eyes unclouded by the memory of the violent clashes.

"And now, you will come to collect yours from Cara. You haven't been in a real battle yet, but we've tried damned hard to give you a realistic idea of the dangers you will face with our various simulations."

Myla's smile grew malicious. She prided herself on the level of cruelty she injected when putting the recruits through their paces. I'd seen my sister unleash two full-size Saurians on one unarmed recruit, only intervening with weaponry after she'd had her arm torn off. "It's character-building for the rest of the class to see what happens to the weak," she had justified, after the recruit in question died from her injuries. On hearing this, Myla had simply shrugged and said, "You can't make an omelette without breaking any eggs."

"But first," Myla continued, "let's raise a glass to you and the future of Galex." The Ys stepped forward to add wine to each recruit's glass. "Congratulations! Be strong, be brave, be ruthless." Each girl chanted the motto back to her before swigging their wine in one gulp, copying Myla's actions.

"Cara, Little Sis," Myla smirked, "have the armour ready."

Laid out to my left was the armour each recruit had earned by passing the six months training programme designed to prepare them to protect and fortify the city walls and fight against our enemy. Their skill set now included shooting, archery, hand-to-hand combat and explosives. With limited weaponry available, they needed to be resourceful. They had been tested to their limits, given tasks to remove empathy and been made to prove they would sacrifice themselves or others for the greater good, if needed. It had been a tough journey for them all, and this evening was in recognition of everything they'd achieved. Their armour shone brightly, and each body suit was carved with the Galex symbol: a fist held over the heart and the words: 'Protector of Galex City'.

As the recruits came up one by one, I passed across their new breastplates, a badge of honour in Galex. Anyone wearing one was treated with respect – all citizens knew what it stood for. As the girls took their suits from me, they smiled shyly, or thanked me quietly. Tyra whispered, "This is because of you, Cara. Thank you for everything."

Her journey had been particularly challenging: she'd started as the underdog, quite physically weak and emotionally sensitive. Myla had been all for dispatching her from the programme early on during one of her visits to the training ground. I'd stuck with her though, sensing she had more to offer. With extra training, support from the other girls and mentoring from me, she'd come on in leaps and bounds.

I always felt proud at these ceremonies: like a lioness watching her cubs bring down a gazelle for the first time. Tonight, though, a shadow flickered across my mind – I knew what these girls would soon face. I also knew that not all of them would survive.

*

Then

The official definition of a 'Saurian' is a 'suborder of lizard' or an 'extinct form that resembles a lizard'. When the Epidemic first emerged, it took a while for people to realise what was going on. At first, death rates just shot up, and the whole world was locked down to try and stop the spread of infection. Roads lay empty, shops were barricaded, and military organisations and police patrolled the streets, forcing the public to remain at home. Because of this, it's unclear when the first mutation occurred. Documents from the time remain, but to begin with, sightings of reptilian beasts were ridiculed – it was thought that being shut away and isolated for long periods of time had sent people round the bend.

Soon though, more and more reports came through and people began to recognise the genuine threat. Not to mention that these creatures didn't really respect boundaries, or concepts such as private property. More and more news reports emerged of people being viciously ripped apart, of their houses being attacked and whole groups murdered.

Of course, people panicked. The men were already dying by the thousand, and now this. No one had yet made the link between the Ys and the mutations. The initial reaction was to try to flee – get away, as far as possible, and hope that neither the virus nor these new monsters followed. Of course, that became a massacre, as Ys trying to escape started mutating. In the past, people lived together in what were called 'family units' – often a man, a woman, and maybe some kids. I'm sure you can see where this is going. Fathers transformed and mutilated their own families. Some photographs from newspapers survive – the images are horrendous. Bodies began piling up – which these creatures fed on. Their loved ones, dead in an instant at their own hands.

They gained the title of 'Saurians' when some scientists decided that the virus must alter the Y chromosome to create a hybrid between human and lizard. There wasn't much time for research into the creatures, or to try and treat those afflicted. They filled the cities: they ravaged towns; they destroyed villages. Those who stayed alive did so by hiding and simply hanging on: surviving. Bomb shelters, some over 100 years old, became safe havens, as did sewers. But so many died. Even more were killed when the bombs came.

It's hard to justify what happened when you've seen the consequences. But I suppose when your towns and cities are overrun by strong, dangerous killing machines, difficult decisions have to be made.

So they were.

About two weeks after the realisation that men were becoming beasts, the remaining government in charge acted. It was called 'strategic bombing'. Any area with high levels of Saurian life-forms was designated a red zone. Alerts were given to allow citizens a chance to flee, but that's easier said than done when hordes of monsters fill the streets. Many simply gave up, accepted their fate. I suppose a bomb seems like a quick escape to oblivion when your life is a living nightmare. Many of the red zones were cities, so casualty numbers were inevitably high. Things weren't much safer in other parts of the country though: it doesn't take huge numbers of Saurians to wreak havoc. In simple terms, there seemed to be a stark choice for most: death by explosives or death by beast.

Other countries followed a similar plan of action. Overnight, it seemed the world became a dried, burnt landscape. Everything was destroyed. Buildings. Parks. Cars. A lot of things I've only seen in pictures, or films, or only know from hearsay. Even now, many things haven't fully returned. Nature is fighting back and reclaiming areas with grass and trees emerging, but it's a slow process. Galex still largely looks like a war zone, with wreckage in the streets and craters in the ground. When most of your population is destroyed in days, there's not so many left to rebuild.

*

Now

Once Myla finally felt she had said enough, and with the armour having been distributed and donned, the recruits were ready to spill out into the night, faces flushed with excitement at their future.

"Should we tell them about the plan for advancement?" Myla murmured in my ear, having slunk over to me now the evening was drawing to a close.

"No," I replied. "Let them have tonight off from thinking about fighting and killing and dying. There'll be time enough for that tomorrow." If this was a coming-of-age experience for them, I wanted them – no, needed them – to enjoy it. At least for one night.

"When they find out they'll be heading up an expedition to find and terminate all Saurians in the outlying towns and villages, they'll realise pretty quickly that it's a suicide mission."

"Hardly," scoffed Myla, "not if you've trained them as efficiently as you say you have. Anyway," she turned her chestnut eyes on mine. "You'll be leading them. If it's suicide for them, it is for you, too."

My stomach turned. She was right, of course. This mission was more dangerous than any we had attempted so far. Our main role to date had been protecting the city. We ensured no creature could breach the walls. We picked off any sole invaders – a brave or foolish Saurian would periodically sidle up to the gates, or a small gaggle would approach with the intent of climbing over. They lacked organisation though, so were easy to defeat. Of course, the work wasn't without risk: even three grown Saurians were a fearsome prospect, which is why we trained the girls so hard. They had to be ready, had to be able to fight a bigger, stronger enemy, and survive.

But this mission – to actively go out and hunt them down, aiming to destroy them completely … this was something new. And dangerous. And daunting.

"Well, obviously I'm hoping to return," I replied, holding her penetrating stare. "But being realistic? We are going to lose a lot of soldiers. A lot of these girls will be dead in two weeks' time."

"We knew the risks when we took this city over," Myla said, slinging her arm over my shoulder. "Remember Mum's advice – never trust a Y. If some of these girls die protecting the next generation from these Y-transformed creatures, then I'd say it's a worthy sacrifice. It's why we decided to train more recruits than ever before – we knew they wouldn't all be coming back. "

With that, she patted my back before making her way out.

"That's fine if you don't have a relationship with the recruits," I murmured to myself. "Helps you to feel less guilty."

The strange thing was – this mission had been *my* idea. My plan to make the world a better place, to expand our territory and provide our community with long-term security. The Y runners sent out regularly to scout the areas around the city were bringing back worrying news. The Saurians were becoming more structured: they were starting to plan, developing in ways we hadn't seen before. If they got organised, if they attacked with force … Well, it wasn't worth thinking about.

And, of course, I'd volunteered to lead the army that would counter-attack before they had time to build in strength. I owed that to my city. I owed that to my sister, who had always kept me safe. It was unthinkable at the time that I wouldn't go. I had to set an example, lead from the front.

What I hadn't counted on, though, was that I wouldn't be doing it alone. I hadn't counted on the fact that two weeks ago, I would discover I was pregnant.

I'd be going into battle, very likely to my death, whilst carrying a baby inside me.

TWO

Waking early the next morning, a wave of sickness flooded me. I rolled out of bed clutching my stomach and made it to the toilet before retching into the bowl. Thankfully, my status meant I had my own quarters with a private bathroom.

Once I'd stopped gagging, I needed to eat. I grabbed a long t-shirt and leggings, cupping a hand over my swelling stomach. So far, no one had noticed it expanding and I'd been careful to only wear baggy clothes, but I knew I wouldn't be able to hide the growing bulge for long. Myla was sharp: she noticed everything. I couldn't risk her finding out.

I guessed I was around 19 weeks pregnant. I could feel the life forming inside me. I was exhausted, with sickness lasting long past the morning and my emotions going haywire. I also had no clue what to do. Who could I tell? Who could I trust with a secret which, if betrayed, would almost certainly lead to the death of this child?

*

Then

My mother was part of a group which survived the bombs that rained down on the city, named by future generations as the Founders. She used to tell us about how we hid underground in the city sewers like rats, listening to the bangs and explosions destroying our home, eating the real rats who tried to escape too. We weren't alone – the most resilient all emerged when the skies went quiet. There was a smallish bunch of them who banded together – all Xs – and they found themselves largely alone in the once beautiful city. At first, they waited for rescue. Surely those who had caused the devastation would come looking for survivors? To help as many caught up in the blasts as they could? But nothing.

Mum told us the story so many times, it almost feels like my own memory, even though I was too young for it to register. The first weeks were spent in the shadows, scrabbling to find food, warmth and shelter. Burnt out vehicles littered the streets, as did human bodies. Rubble, smoke, smashed glass, oil, tyres, scrap metal – only a bleak landscape remained. The fear of surviving Saurians shrouded the group – they'd seen the beasts up close and suspected even the fire-power unleashed wouldn't have destroyed them all. There was also the worry that some Ys might have survived as we had, and they could still transform if infected.

It became clear that there was to be no rescue. No saviours. Those who had survived were on their own. As is often the case, someone took charge. Here, it was an X named Gloria. Tall, blonde and muscular, she seemed the obvious choice for leader. As a former Royal Marine, (this was like a super-tough soldier, mum explained), she decided the most important thing to do first was find a base which could be defended against attack. So, they went looking for somewhere sturdy, that hadn't been too damaged in the blasts, with plenty of space. The discovery of an old school first built in the 1800s seemed perfect – by some miracle, it was largely untouched with lots of generous spaces and even a fully equipped kitchen. It had been a boarding school, so there were dormitories too, and a gated wall. Ideal to hole up in.

Gloria allocated jobs quickly and efficiently. Some were sent to loot food from supermarkets, some to find bedding, others to clear the living spaces. She took a couple to source weapons. Mum said they managed to find some guns from who knows where, but mostly they were reliant on spears, clubs, knives and anything else they could cobble together from the debris lying around. From then on, they sat tight, and survived. The Founders had unknowingly set up a new community, small as it currently was.

As time passed, more wanderers came. Some stayed. Others simply rested before moving on, usually in some hopeless quest to find family.

At times, even Ys came for refuge. Most of the survivors called for their deaths – they were too dangerous, like ticking time-bombs. Gloria resisted though – she chose to lock them up and study them, supported by Shylah, a former scientist. The hope was that a cure for either the virus or the mutations could be found, or at the very least, a greater understanding of the Epidemic established. That way, they might be able to prevent it from taking hold again. This was probably a more appealing prospect for the Ys than for the Xs. Between the prospect of an antidote and a very real fear of what they could become, most were happy to undertake imprisonment. Any that weren't were simply denied access to our safe haven.

Things became more confusing when women with children arrived at the school. One was pregnant with twins, whilst another had two boys under three. Could children be treated as a threat too? So far, there was no evidence that the virus even affected kids – it seemed likely that puberty changed this, making Ys susceptible at around thirteen years old. So, the boys were allowed to stay, and live amongst the wider community, exempt from the restrictions placed upon older Ys. Of course, some had reservations, but those who'd lost sons or brothers particularly, clung to the hope that a different future could be found for these children. They posed no real danger – for now.

*

Now

Making my way down to the dinner hall for breakfast, hoping I wouldn't hurl anything else back up, I made a decision. I had to confide in someone. At some point soon, I was going to need help to hide my expanding waistline. The only person I trusted was Ilana. We'd grown up together and been close for as long as I could remember. I could trust her with my life – and now, I needed to.

As I ladled out a bowl of wholegrain porridge and sprinkled in dried berries, I scanned the room for my friend.

The warriors of the city still lived in the original school building – it was like our headquarters. There was plenty of space for us and the Y slaves, who were mainly based here too. Pouring a coffee, I spotted Ilana in the corner, deep in conversation with Myla. They both glanced at me as I made my way over, and a shadow seemed to flicker over Myla's face, if just for a second, before she turned on her heels and marched out of the hall.

"Hey," I smiled, plopping down opposite Ilana before taking a large gulp from my drink.

"Hey you!" she replied, her toothy grin a welcome sight.

"What's up with Myla?"

"Oh, you know," she sighed, sounding a little uncomfortable. "We were just discussing the planned expedition."

My stomach dropped. This was why I had to share my secret soon – in a few weeks, I would be heading up a team venturing out on the most dangerous mission ever attempted. Ilana was my second-in-command – we had meticulously planned the assault together. Her knowledge of the Saurians was unparalleled: she studied the creatures, taking a scientific interest in their genetic make-up. She was also a fearsome soldier. This attack had been both our brainchild. I didn't want to let her down, but I had no other option – I certainly couldn't tell Myla. I was either going to have to get out of the mission somehow, or go, and hope my friend would be able to shield me from the worst of the danger.

"Any further plans made?" I asked lightly. Ilana shifted her blue eyes away from mine and brushed her short black hair back behind her ear – a gesture which told me she felt guilty about something.

"Just that Myla thinks we should take some of the Ys with us – you know, runners, hunters. She reckons they could be useful. And by useful, she means as bait, a sacrifice or a human shield."

Ilana counted these options off on her fingers as she spoke, mimicking the heartless tone Myla always adopted when discussing anything Y-related.

"She genuinely seems okay with the idea of letting Ys die if it keeps the recruits safe." She dropped her voice low, in case of eavesdroppers.

"I see." Now it was my turn to slide my eyes away from hers. "Can we get out of here? Go for a quick run before training starts?"

"Of course," Ilana replied, looking at me with concern.

I realised I couldn't wait much longer to talk to her, now that sacrificing Ys had become part of the plan. One of those Ys was the father of my baby. And I was in love with him.

*

Then

It took a while, but this small group of strangers, the Founders, managed to form a new community. The school provided relative safety, and foraging from burnt-out shops kept up a fairly steady supply of food and other necessities. As suspected, some Saurians had survived the bombings – but numbers were generally small and with so few remaining, they didn't seem to grow rapidly. Before long, the Founders grew more confident and started to reclaim the city beyond the school gates. It was decided that a new city could be created – and from this, the idea of Galex was born. Mum reckons the name started as a joke – apparently 'gal' was a patronising way of referring to an X in the past. With heavy irony, the city would be Gal followed by the X, which had proven to be the strongest chromosome. Gloria thought it would be funny to name the city Galex, like a finger being stuck up to anyone who had ever thought Xs were the weaker sex.

Obviously, not everyone had initially been on board with the zero-tolerance approach to Ys. Those who disagreed had largely moved on, some even taking their menfolk with them. I guess they couldn't let go of loved ones. I still thought of them sometimes, hoped things had worked out for them. My head told me that the reality had probably often been brutal and bloody, but my heart imagined a simple family life for them in some isolated part of the country.

The women who remained in Galex, though, they were characterised by something else: they were haunted by some kind of experience involving a Y. Many had seen loved ones transform, seen husbands and fathers become monsters. Some had lost children to their hands. Others had simply been attacked by strangers. Whatever they'd seen, whatever they'd felt – each had first-hand experience of how dangerous a Y could become, in an instant.

These ingrained memories taught the citizens of Galex that protection was vital, so a plan was hatched to erect a wall of some sort to form a border around this new city –

smaller than the previous one, but built right at the heart of the old town. This space had everything that was needed to survive: plenty of shops to ransack, a water source, space where hopefully grass and crops could flourish again. There were raw materials aplenty to build a wall – shifting the rubble, bricks and mortar from the explosions would not only help clear the streets, but could easily be piled up to create fortifications. The question left was: who would build it?

The answer led to another change in this blossoming society. The Ys. By now, the group of Xs stood at about 130, with around 25 Ys under lock and key. Why not use them? They were being kept alive, being given precious rations – why not make them earn their keep? And so, the wall was slowly, but surely, built up around an area approximately five miles square. It was no mean feat and took several years. It also cost a couple of the older Ys their lives. The end result, though, became a symbol of safety to everyone encased inside.

Mum always said that the early years were golden. She loved seeing Myla and me grow up, and the new city of Galex started to feel like home. People formed friendships and bonds. Some even started relationships. The presence of children gave hope for a future. The kids used to play in the school grounds together – even the Y children were permitted to join in. I suppose a few of the women got broody, because the next idea was how to make more babies. Questions were raised, of course. Was it safe? Would they get infected? How would they go about it?

Obviously, I know how babies are made – but this was

different. To have a relationship with a Y seemed unthinkable – the virus was still veiled in mystery, and no one really knew if there would be a resurgence. It was decided that letting a Y out was simply too risky.

It was Shylah who came up with a solution. As a scientist, she had been busy studying the Ys as best she could, using the school's lab resources. She took blood samples, put them through fitness tests, anything she could think of to understand their physical make-up better. Ultimately, she was looking for a cure – she had lost her whole family before the bombs even fell. Mum guessed that she wanted to think things could go back to the way they were before, and that a cure might make that a possibility.

She realised that if she was already taking blood samples, she could take other types of samples too – and so, the Galex Sperm Bank was born. It was pretty clinical – the hopeful mothers-to-be would come down to the labs, have a look at the Ys up close and then select a matching sample. Shylah helped them as much as possible with ovulation kits looted from pharmacies, to give them the best chance of conceiving. The first time it happened, Mum said there was such joy that the celebrations lasted for days. Successes continued, and patterns emerged, as some Ys had a better success rate than others.

Soon, more and more women became pregnant. They were blooming, and it seemed wonderful – the human race would continue and could thrive again! Babies started to be delivered. A great deal survived, and the world really began to seem like a hopeful place again. Everything seemed brighter: the destruction from the bombs was diminishing and futures were being planned. Memories of mutations faded, even if they remained ever-present shadows in the corners of the mind, making the danger posed by the virus seem less urgent. It became a relic from the past rather than a modern day threat.

A decision was made: the Ys had given something so special in helping society to procreate, they deserved a second chance. Consequently, the community came to a new agreement: the Ys would no longer be imprisoned, but instead would be free to live as part of the group. Family units started to take shape again and for many, the world seemed to right itself.

You've probably realised by now that this happy utopia didn't last. It ended abruptly one morning when my mother went down to Shylah's laboratory. She found the walls stained with blood. Following the trail to the store cupboard, she found Shylah – or what was left of her. She said what really hit her was the smell, like rotten eggs. Sulphur. She had smelled this before – in the street when she had killed a Saurian who was about to attack her daughter.

There seemed to be only two ways to explain what was happening. Either a Saurian had invaded the community, or – one of the Ys had mutated.

*

Now

"So, what's up?" Ilana inquired gently, as we jogged around the circumference of the city walls.

I slowed to a walk. "I need to tell you something. It's big." I looked at her, scratching the back of my head as I always did when I was nervous.

She slowed her pace too. "Okay … is it the mission? Are you having second thoughts?"

"Not exactly. It's just not going to be as straightforward as we first thought."

Ilana stopped now and looked at me, shielding her eyes from the sun. She waited. I realised I'd have to just take the plunge and say it.

"I'm going to have a baby." The words dropped like stones. Now out there, there was no taking them back.

*

Then

I was nine when Shylah was murdered and things changed forever. Despite being young, I remember it all really clearly. The following events were a huge part of Galex's history and changed the entire fabric of our city. Graffitied murals depict events, a bit like stained-glass windows in churches portraying stories from the bible. Once a year, we light candles to remember what happened. Shylah's memorial still inspires today's scientists to continue her work of finding a cure for the Epidemic. It's become an event that defines us; that we've learnt from.

Initially though, it seemed panic took over. Alarms were rung. The community was gathered together, head counts were done.

It didn't take long to work out that with two Ys missing, we were dealing with two new mutations. Both were fathers and had been living with partners in the community. It wasn't clear why they might have been in Shylah's laboratory, but vials left out suggested she was planning to collect blood samples. Maybe they'd had symptoms of the disease and were seeking advice when something had triggered their mutation, or maybe Shylah had been experimenting with a new drug or treatment. It no longer mattered. The priority now was to find and destroy the beasts before they could cause any more damage.

Of course, it wasn't that simple. The community had become complacent. The world had seemed safer, so few felt prepared to take on two dangerous foes with their limited weaponry. It fell to the Founders to find and kill the creatures – after all, they had proven their strength and leadership by setting up this new society. It felt only right that they stepped forward to prevent its destruction.

Once the remaining Ys had been safely locked away again, the rest of the community took refuge in the old school gym. The doors were barricaded with whatever could be found: chairs, tables, desks. Lights off, everyone gathered in the middle of the room and endeavoured to stay as quiet as possible.

Hours passed. We remained hidden, shivering in fear. In the dark, our sense of hearing went into hyperdrive. We heard screams. Shrieks. Clashes. Crashes. Roars. The noises continued, including some banging caused by something trying to break down the doors that protected us, until at last, all went silent.

We waited. Afraid to find out what would confront us beyond the doors, we stayed still for a long time. In the end, a weak knocking got us moving.

One of the older girls approached the door. "Password?"

"Double double, toil and trouble."

We scrabbled to unblock the door and let the survivor in.

Turned out it was survivors. Staggering through the doors, Gloria tumbled in. She part-carried, part-dragged our mother, who was alive, but barely. She had severe wounds – slashes across her entire body from claws, the cuts all edged with a bluish sticky substance. Saurian venom. We know she had mere hours to live.

"The others?" someone asked.

Gloria shook her head. "It took all of us to bring them down. I'm the last one standing."

Mum was quickly moved to the sick bay where we were allowed to see her for the last time. She looked so pale and small in the crisp white bed. She beckoned Myla and me closer.

"Stay strong," she croaked. "Don't let us have died for nothing. Protect them. Look after each other." She leaned back, head drooping onto her pillow, fighting for shallow breaths. I thought that was it. Head in hands, I suddenly felt a vice-like grip on my wrist. Mum had grabbed me, her eyes wide and angry.

"And do not trust the Ys."

She flopped back again, arms dropping. Her eyes shut. She was gone.

*

Now

"You're *what*? That's not … But that's impossible!" Ilana was breathing hard, and not just because she had been running. She looked at me wildly, and I could see fear and something else in her eyes. Disappointment?

"I know it's a shock –"

"A shock?! That's a complete understatement! Why didn't you tell me you'd been trying? Does Myla know you accessed the Sperm Bank?"

Okay, here came the tricky part. The unforgivable part.

"I didn't," I murmured. I stared at Ilana until the penny dropped.

"Shit! Does that mean …?" She couldn't say the words – sleeping with a Y was unthinkable. Forbidden. Especially for the sister of Galex's leader.

I nodded imperceptibly. "I'm in trouble."

"You think? Flipping heck! What are we going to do?"

I burst into tears. Partly because I was afraid, and so didn't know how to answer her. But also, partly because she'd said 'we'.

Ilana hugged me. "It'll be ok," she replied. "I can help you." She pulled back and looked at me hard. "You going to tell me who got you into this pickle?"

"Does it matter?" I smiled ruefully.

She shrugged. "I guess not. Although I really wouldn't want to be in his shoes when Myla finds out. Does he know?"

"Not yet. That's my next job."

*

Then

After Shylah, things changed dramatically in Galex. The dead Founders were buried in the school grounds, with a sombre memorial speech from Gloria. She stayed in control, but the whole structure of our society was altered. The old system was simply considered too dangerous.

Gloria started training up the younger girls in combat. Days spent running around and playing games were now filled with military exercises, assault courses and archery. Gloria was insistent that we were equipped to defend, or attack, against any threat.

Myla proved a very willing combatant – she took Mum's death hard, and threw herself into the new regime. In a few years she made lieutenant, then captain. It seemed inevitable she would take over from Gloria when she stepped down and it was clear she would continue the same focus. I don't think either of them realised how soon that would be, though.

That wasn't the only change. Any freedoms the Ys had been granted were swiftly removed. Whereas Gloria had once taught kindness, cruelty was now the order of the day. She seemed to blame each individual Y for the trauma suffered – even the children. It was as if she no longer saw them as human – they were simply potential monsters that you must never turn your back on.

She wasn't alone in this way of thinking – people were angry and afraid. The Ys became the scapegoats for the slaughter of our Founders. Any disobedience was swiftly and brutally punished. Fear led decisions, and the Ys grew to fear all Xs.

The only reason Gloria didn't slaughter them all was the need to keep making babies. Shylah had been training up several other girls in the labs so there was no problem with the Sperm Bank, or with the continued search for a vaccine. Instead, the Ys were demoted to the status of slaves. Their identities were removed: instead of names, they were assigned a number and a colour, dependent on their job. New roles were dished out to them now that the Xs' time was taken training – they did the cleaning, cooking, maintenance around the school and any communal areas in the city. There was a strict chain of command, with all Ys reporting to an allocated X. The older Ys were sent out into the city to bring back supplies, or to hunt, and later, beyond the wall to scout out the surrounding terrain. They were called runners – their purpose being to return with intelligence about any Saurian threat, any other civilisations that had survived, or just general information about what was out there. They didn't always come back. We could never be sure if they were killed or simply decided to make their own way.

And could you blame them? Their choices were bleak. Stay, and be a slave, feared and hated. Go, and risk either mutating into a beast, or being killed by the monsters that roamed free. Ultimately, life in Galex was so grim that some must have thought that death was at least a way out. Or maybe, in a strange way, the thought of transforming into a mindless creature was freeing.

The family units that had started to take shape again now disappeared forever. The babies kept coming, but now Xs were raised by the community, destined to become warriors to protect the city. Any Ys simply joined the ranks of the slaves. No one had a 'mother' anymore – this concept was lost in the new, harder world order.

For Myla, I think this was a relief – she missed Mum so much, that seeing other people fulfil this role would have felt like salt in a wound. She shut herself off emotionally, blaming all Ys for her pain. We were still close and she was as protective over me as ever, but something was missing. I feared her spark, her empathy, was gone for good.

For me? I missed Mum too, missed her hugs, our closeness. But I yearned to feel that love again.

THREE

With Ilana behind me and the weight of my secret finally lifted, I felt surprisingly upbeat as I showered before heading off to the training ground. I expected a few of the recruits to have sore heads after their celebrations last night. They would soon sober up when we told them what was planned for the next few months. Then, after that, I had another task – tell the father about the baby.

Setting off to the training ground, I bumped into Myla, also heading there.

"All ready?" she inquired.

"As I'll ever be," I replied. "Are you sure you want me to tell them?"

"Yes," she answered decisively. "You came up with the plan. Anyway, they trust you."

She had a point. Myla might be in charge, but to these

girls, I was the authority. It was me who had pushed them, demanding blood, sweat and tears. I'd encouraged them as they improved and scolded them if they slacked off. I'd dished out pep talks, advice and orders. I was probably the closest thing to a mother they had, or would ever have.

Walking through the city, I marvelled at how much it had changed. That dream the Founders had, of crops and grass? It had come true. Things were tidy, and there was even trade happening again. It was amazing how enterprising people could be: I saw the shells of cars transformed into beautiful garden areas and vegetable patches, or even changed into benches. Myla might be hard-faced, I thought, but she had really helped turn the place around. Those who were deemed too weak to be protectors were put to use elsewhere, given different skills. And, of course, the Y slaves were extra labour for jobs that really needed doing.

When we arrived at the training ground, the girls were already hard at work. Some did look a bit ropey after last night, but none of them wanted to be the weakest link, so they were all putting in that little bit of extra effort to hide the fact that they weren't feeling 100%. I smiled inwardly, knowing I would be putting my game face on today, too.

Ilana had beaten me here and was already engaged in combat-training with Becka. She waved at me, but I noticed her smile faded when she realised Myla was with me. I wondered if there was something going on between the two of them – this was the second time she'd looked uncomfortable in her presence.

"Morning, Protectors," I shouted, watching with pride as the recruits quickly laid down their weapons and saluted.

"Glad to see you all made it through the night unscathed!" They giggled.

"I want to congratulate you again on your achievements – getting to where you are has been no mean feat – not everyone is up to it. You've proven yourselves to be the best of the best." The faces in front of me beamed with pride. Tyra looked like she would burst she was so pleased. Here, I paused, gearing myself up for the next announcement.

"Which is why we," I gestured at myself and Myla, "feel you are ready for your next challenge." A hum of voices broke out as the recruits excitedly turned to one another, eager to find out what was coming next.

"You've probably noticed, as have we, that with our growing population, Galex has become a little bit cosy."

Laughter again. It felt like we lived on top of each other like sardines crammed in a tin behind the city walls. With higher birth-rates and a safe atmosphere, Galex had more people living in it than ever before. "And we're hoping you might just be our solution."

"You're not going to sacrifice us to bring the numbers down, are you?" quipped Lola, one of the more popular girls, a mock-horrified look on her pretty face. They laughed again – but already an edge of nervousness was creeping in. I guessed they were picking up on my reluctance, despite my best efforts to keep my tone breezy.

"Sacrifice our brightest? Never!" A sigh of relief seemed to float up to the sky. "But we do need your help." They looked at me expectantly.

"We need to expand the city. Your job will be to clear the surrounding areas of any threats," Myla spoke up. I looked at her, angry that she had butted in and spoken so bluntly. I'd hoped she'd let me deliver the news in a slightly softer way. Last week, we'd heard the runners' reports about groups of Saurians congregating and nesting a mile or so outside the city walls. This was dangerous in itself – if they attacked, they could kill a lot of citizens. We needed to get out in front and strike first, especially if these creatures were evolving in the way we suspected.

The runners were perhaps our most valuable Ys. Made up of the fastest and bravest, they were sent out frequently to explore the surrounding terrain. They often brought valuable information about nearby dangers like Saurian nests, or potential new food sources. In exchange for their usefulness, they tended to be shielded from the worst treatment dished out by Myla. They also got extra rations and more time off than any other category of Y.

"What do you mean, threats?" Tyra asked, nervously rebraiding her hair. "Do you mean Ys? Or Saurians?"

"Both," Myla barked back. "We need the area. We need to dismantle the current city walls and expand out. Anything in our way will have to be destroyed. We can't risk taking any more Ys: we're already dangerously close to capacity. If they tried to fight back –"

"They won't," I murmured, "if you treat them fairly." She shot me a glance I couldn't read.

The recruits looked anxious, as well they should. Their solemn faces told me they understood what was being asked of them. They knew as well as we did that this was a dangerous mission. We all felt relatively safe behind the walls: picking off the odd Saurian, or targeting a small group just outside the wall was one thing, but knowingly walking into a nest? With potentially other, bigger nests nearby? It was asking for trouble.

"Look," I said, taking care to make as much eye contact as I could. "I know how it sounds. But I'll be with you. And so will Ilana. We'll take weapons, as many as we can carry; we'll have hunters and runners to support us, too. And we're not going tomorrow – now you know the plan, we can focus our training on how to deal with the situations we might face. I'm not asking anything of you that I won't be doing myself. Our city needs this. It's the right thing to do."

A lot of the recruits nodded. It made sense. And if we weren't going to do it, then who? We were the strong. The others looked up to us.

I just wish that it didn't feel so wrong.

*

Then

The world I'd known before my mum died seemed long gone. I had vague memories of playtime, of laughing with Ys and of a Myla before she forgot how to smile. A part of me still missed it – I suppose it felt like my childhood ended early, and the sadness I felt was a loss of my innocence as well as the loss of our way of life.

Perhaps inevitably, things were tougher after the Saurian attack and the deaths of the Founders. Gloria was tougher, Myla was tougher – and, I suppose to an extent, I was tougher. As I grew older, I threw myself into training. Before long, it became clear that I had real talent. By the time I turned 13,

I could beat anyone at hand-to-hand combat. My archery scores were nearly always the highest. On the shooting range, I never missed. I'm not boasting – it's a fact. I think I had to channel my grief into something, so I chose this, and kept working and working at it until I became the best.

I suppose it wasn't that surprising that Gloria noticed my skill, or that Myla was jealous. As her younger sister, I looked up to her in every way, but it must have been a bit galling to see me doing so well, especially when she'd always been the golden girl. Even worse to see me starting to catch Gloria's eye.

"You have leadership potential," she started telling me. "You could run this city one day."

Of course, I was flattered. Having someone as powerful as Gloria respect me felt amazing. I lapped up her attention. She started mentoring me herself, not just in terms of my physical fitness, but in terms of explaining how Galex was run, who she trusted, how the systems worked.

The sticking point, though, was my sister. Her brown eyes practically turned green with envy every time she caught sight of Gloria and me together. She tried to gain her attention with stunts, like the public punishment of a Y who brought her the wrong sort of tea. This backfired by making her seem a bit erratic though and, in fact, pushed Gloria more towards me. Also, Gloria seemed less hard than she had in the immediate aftermath of the Saurian attack. Her anger and bitterness towards the Ys had mellowed somewhat: she perhaps remembered that they were victims too. Not to Myla, though. Nothing could change her views, so damaged had she been by her experiences.

About six months after she really took an interest in me, Gloria sat both me and Myla down. She laid out her plans for the future.

"I won't be here forever," she began, "and I need people I can trust to take this place forward. I've heard of another city set-up, further south. Amex, it's called. It's pretty different to here, more liberal."

"We've tried that route," interrupted Myla impatiently. "Look where leniency got us. Dead." She sat back and crossed her arms, as if to say, end of conversation.

Gloria smiled tightly. "I remember vividly," she said tartly, one eyebrow raised. "But if they have managed to find a way to live with more equality, I think it's worth pursuing. There's even rumours that they are close to a cure."

"I don't care about equality!" Myla yelled. "As far as I'm concerned, Ys killed my mother. And countless others. They don't deserve to live among us."

"And that attitude is the reason I've brought you both here today," Gloria sighed. "I am going to travel to Amex and see how they run things. I will, if possible, be bringing back ideas about how we can improve our community. If there's even a chance we can live together like we used to, it's worth taking the risk. You won't remember the past clearly before the Epidemic, but I do. I had a husband – a Y – and he was and still is the best person I've ever met. It's not their fault that this virus attacks them." Gloria paused, before continuing.

"I'll admit I was angry, and scared. But now's the time to see if we can build a better world."

"How do you even know about this place, Amex?" Myla spat. She was seething – I'd never seen her so full of rage.

39

"I sent out a group of runners to go further than we've ventured before. They heard about it from a group of Ys on their way there. They welcome everyone."

"Why are you telling us this now?" I asked.

"My plan is to take a small group of recruits and find my way to this city. Whilst I'm away, I need you two to take over here and make sure things run smoothly, make sure everyone stays safe. You're my two best warriors after all."

"You don't want us to come with you?" Myla questioned, looking dismayed.

"No. You're too valuable and the risk is too high. If for some reason I don't return, I need you to take control permanently. My plan is to take a couple of runners and send them back at various points along the way to keep you informed of our progress."

"How will us being in charge work?" I asked.

"Not us – you," Gloria said, looking pointedly at me. "You will assume the leadership. Myla, of course you will have an important role too – that of City Protector. You will train the recruits and support Cara in her new role."

I couldn't look at Myla. Her eyes were boring into my skull and I could sense bitterness, imagining a flush of shame rising across her cheeks. Of course she would feel overlooked. It would be a slap in the face to be seconded by anyone – but her *younger* sister?

"Why her? Why not me?" she asked petulantly.

"Cara has a more level-headed character," Gloria said honestly. "She'll be the more temperate leader. Your skills lie on the battlefield."

"She's not ready," Myla urged, kneeling before Gloria.

"She can't see the dangers to us all. She can't do what needs to be done. I can." Her chin jutted stubbornly. "I will risk everything to protect this community."

Gloria sighed, taking Myla's hands. "But that may be the problem," she told her softly. "A leader can't just see the world in black and white. Wrong and right. Bad and good. It's full of anomalies, exceptions. That beautiful grey where good and evil merge. Cara recognises that. You don't."

"Whatever," Myla responded sullenly, before stalking out of the room.

I must have looked worried because Gloria reassured me, "She'll come around. Deep down, she knows it's the right path."

She was wrong.

*

Now

The rest of the training session passed without incident, despite a generally subdued air. I could tell some of the girls were dubious – no doubt there would be plenty of dormitory discussions between them tonight. I also sensed that they would go along with the plan, though. They'd given me their all – they wouldn't desert me now, despite the dangers. If they had to, they would put their lives on the line, as would I. It just felt more complicated now it wasn't only my life.

"Cara!"

I turned to see Ilana jogging up to me, her long legs striding comfortably across the ground.

"Hang on," she panted. "Are you still planning to go on the mission? Is that wise?"

It wasn't particularly easy to get pregnant in Galex, so pregnant women were usually protected from anything that might cause harm to the baby. The mother did very little until the baby was born and taken to be raised in the school building, so they could be studied to see where their talents lay. If anyone found out I was carrying a child, my career would be over.

"I don't know, Ilana," I sighed. "To be honest, I've not even got my head around it all yet."

"It is crazy. I really can't imagine how Myla will take it."

I stopped and grabbed hold of her arms. "You cannot tell her, under any circumstances. I can't let her take this baby."

My hand went to my stomach. I hadn't even realised that was what I was going to say. I'd thought my worries had been about my job – but I understood for the first time just how much I wanted this baby. I could still remember the bond I'd felt with my mother – this could be my chance to feel that again. "Please," I begged.

Ilana took my hands in hers. "Of course. This is your secret. I won't betray you. But –" She shifted uneasily, her eyes anxious against her light brown skin.

"But what?"

"I think Myla suspects … something. I don't know how much exactly, but she's been trying to get me to keep tabs on you and report back."

Suddenly my spine went cold. Did she know? Had she guessed?

"So far, I've just been fobbing her off, making up some stuff about you feeling guilty over the upcoming mission and the fact you might lose some recruits." She shrugged. "I kind of thought that must be the problem. I had no idea about –" she gestured to my stomach.

I exhaled. "Well, if you didn't have any inkling, I can only hope Myla's still clueless, too."

I couldn't shake the feeling that Myla might know more than we thought, though – she was certainly wily, and very used to getting her own way. I was also pretty sure that Ilana wouldn't be the only person she was trying to get to spy on me. Who else couldn't I trust?

*

Then

After Gloria's announcement to Myla and me, my sister barely spoke to me for weeks. She threw herself into training and seemed to be trying to ignore the fact that I even existed. Gloria kept up her mentoring of me, only now with increased urgency as we had a clearer time frame of when I would actually take over.

I can still remember Gloria's mission setting off. With two Ys and five recruits, they were a small party going on a long journey. Laden with rucksacks filled with supplies and tents, they clambered over the wall, waving madly to us. I remember thinking they looked full of possibility. Even the Ys had hope stamped on their faces.

It was two days later when the recruits returned. They had a haunted look about them, as if something terrible had happened.

The tallest of them, Amina, told us her version of what had taken place – the others simply nodded along as she spoke.

In her story, she had woken to find Gloria covered in blood having been stabbed as she slept. The knife was found inside the two Ys' tent. Realising they must have murdered her, Amina killed them in her rage. The rest of the recruits awoke to find three bodies. Deciding to give the mission up as a lost cause, they returned home, having buried Gloria's body on the edge of a forest.

"When I got to her, she did have some last words," Amina claimed. "She said she'd made a mistake thinking we could live in a more equal society. Ys were dangerous. Myla was right, so it should be her to take charge of Galex."

And so, it came to be that Myla took over, and I took her job as Protector. It wasn't long before she started treating the Ys even worse, and any plan to get to Amex was abandoned. Amina was given a position of power as Myla's advisor. However, after about six months, she disappeared – where to, nobody ever found out. Myla had some tale about her wanting to see what else was out there beyond the walls. She said she'd fancied herself as a bit of an explorer and had wanted to go it alone on an adventure.

I imagine you're thinking what I suspected. The whole thing was planned by Myla. Get rid of Gloria, using Amina as some kind of pawn to gain power. Once Amina had done her job, she was no longer useful and could be a risk – what if she talked? Or demanded more in return for her silence? So, she had to go, too.

I thought back to that terrified little girl hiding behind her mother's legs, as she watched her younger sister need rescuing from a Saurian. That innocence and fear had gone, warped by pain and loss and hatred. Could my sister be ruthless enough to have engineered Gloria's murder? To turn on her ally if she became a threat?

I feared the answer to both questions was yes.

*

Now

It was much later that evening when I finally managed to slip out unseen. Being more careful now than ever, I waited until the dormitories had gone quiet and slunk out. There were only a couple of recruits posted to guard the school – Tyra was placed at the nearest exit to me.

"Hey Tyra," I greeted her.

"Hi!" She smiled broadly at me, her teeth pristinely white against the backdrop of her dark face. "You okay?"

"Oh fine," I said, stretching and limbering up, in what I hoped wasn't an over-exaggerated way. "Just can't sleep yet, the mission is whirling around my head. I'm going to try and run it off before bed."

"Good idea," Tyra replied. "I think a lot of the girls are feeling nervous about it. Not that I think you're nervous," she gabbled, not wanting to offend me. "I mean, you're leading us out there so you must know what you're doing."

I smiled wearily. "Well, I hope so," I answered. "Anyway, see you later. I might come in the entrance round the other side, so don't worry if you don't see me again tonight."

"No problem. Enjoy your run," she called, as I started to pick up speed.

Once out of sight, I slowed my pace again. I doubled back into the shadows and crept round to the back of the school complex. Towards the rear were the less impressive quarters – we guessed they must have once housed the least important staff members, like the cooks and gardeners. Either that, or the most unruly pupils were sent there. Shabbier than the main buildings, they were at least private though, with a small kitchen garden that still yielded various herbs and vegetables.

I clambered up the iron railing that separated these quarters – an additional safety measure to keep the Xs and Ys separate – until I was beneath the windows of the largest dormitory, in which 15 Ys slumbered. If I got caught here, directly under the Ys' living area, I'd have some explaining to do. I might be able to stick to my lie about going for a run, but this dark corner was not the most obvious route I could take. Best if I could remain hidden from any prying eyes.

I bent down, grabbed a handful of pebbles and starting to throw them, one by one, against the window on the far left-hand side of the dormitory. Most hit their mark with a subtle tap that could be put down to the wind. After each throw, I stepped back into the alcoves. When three stones struck their target in a row, I glimpsed a light flash off and on, twice. That was our signal. I sidled further around the building and sat on the bench behind the row of fruit trees at the bottom of the garden.

Within minutes, I felt a hand on my shoulder. I was always amazed at how quietly he could creep around. I suppose he had to. We hugged fiercely.

"You okay?" he whispered. I paused to take in his face. A shadow on his chin told me he'd not shaved in a couple of days.

"Yes," I replied. "I just needed to see you." Smiling, his hand cupped my chin and we stared into each other's eyes.

"You look tired."

"We had a long run today," he yawned. "Checking out the southern side. It looks like there might be a big nest down that way." He grinned his lopsided smile. "I'm never too tired to see you, though."

I gripped his hands. "I can't be long. I think Myla is already a bit suspicious around me at the minute. My sister always seems to have a knack of knowing when something's going on."

"You don't think she suspects –" he sounded scared, absent-mindedly running his hand across his stubbly head. I couldn't blame him. If our relationship were discovered, he would be killed. Myla would make an example of him.

"No, no. Not yet. But we are going to have a problem soon." His blue eyes were flecked with grey – they never left mine for a moment.

"First thing. Don't volunteer for any new missions. The attack on the Saurians? It's going ahead in a few weeks. I don't want you to be part of it."

He protested, as I'd known he would.

"I need you here, Brown, keeping yourself safe. Because when I get back, we're going to have a baby."

BROWN

FOUR

Gobsmacked. This is perhaps the best word for how I felt when Cara told me the news. Shocked. Excited. Scared. These emotions followed swiftly after.

"Can you say that again? I'm not sure I heard right." Her green eyes shone in the dark, like a cat's.

"You did hear me," she repeated patiently. "I said we're going to have a baby."

"I did think that's what you said."

We grinned at each other. Even when the stakes were high, she could still make me smile like an idiot.

"You're sure?"

Cara nodded. "I did a test I pinched from the lab. Actually, I did three to make triple sure."

"And … how do you feel? Are you feeling well?" I put my hand to her forehead to test her temperature, the way I remember my mum doing to me.

"I'm not an invalid," she protested, grabbing my hand and squeezing it. "I feel fine! Well, apart from the sickness, but that's starting to fade."

"It's just, well, a bit scary, I guess," she continued. "Knowing what to do next. I needed to tell you as soon as I could. It's a lot to get your head round."

"Well, that's for sure," I replied. I squeezed her hand back. "But for now, you are the most important thing here, and keeping you safe. I don't really know what I can do to help."

And I didn't. In my position, I was fairly useless. Cara was an X. She had the power. She had the big important job, and the big important (though totally psychotic) older sister. I was a nobody. No authority, no voice. All I did was run into danger and back. I was a glorified messenger boy. How could I protect her? And this – our – baby?

"It's tricky, I know," Cara said, her hand moving to stroke my cheek. I gripped it tight – moments like this for us were hard to come by. "For now, I've just got to hide it. I can't risk Myla finding out. I don't know how she would react."

Badly, was the word that sprung to mind. Anything to do with a Y, and Myla always reacted badly.

"Are you … I mean, are we … keeping it?"

She looked at me, this time using both hands to cup my face.

"Yes," she said. "I will do anything to keep this baby. And to keep you safe too."

With that, she kissed me, and any fears I had melted away, if only for that moment.

·   *

Our secret tryst was brief. With patrolling protectors, even this far around the grounds, Cara couldn't stay for long.

After our kiss, she told me not to worry, reminded me not to put myself forward for any missions and then snuck back through the garden.

My head was spinning. I headed back to the dormitory as stealthily as I could. Of course, Blue noticed.

"Where you bin, then, bruv?" His bunk creaked as he turned his bulky frame towards me.

"Just needed a piss," I lied. He was like a brother to me, but I needed some time to process the news myself first before sharing with him.

"'Kay, if you say so." Blue yawned and rolled over again. Pretty soon, a grunting snore rose from his bed.

I kept replaying the conversation with Cara in my head. A baby. Our baby. My stomach flipped. It was unbelievable! We'd only done it once … Could this be happening? It felt unreal.

Possibilities and options whirled through my head, making sleep hard to come by. The restless sleepers around me tossed and turned and I could hear every last movement. By the time I finally drifted off, I knew only one thing for certain: there was no way I was letting Cara go out on a mission without me – whatever else happened, I had to volunteer to be there with her.

*

The morning alarm felt brutal. Bells rang loudly in the dorm every morning at six, giving us time to get up and report for duty. It must have felt the same for those teenage boys who were in the school so many years ago. Just like us, I'm sure they would have been reluctant to leave the warmth of their beds for a day's work. Though, to be honest, I'd do anything to swap my day for one filled with advanced algebra and physics.

After what felt like only five minutes' sleep, I dragged my body up and placed my feet squarely on the cold floor.

"You look like a corpse, bro," joked Blue.

"I feel like one too," I answered, stretching my arms to hear them crack. I padded to the washroom to get cleaned up. Red and Orange were in there already, brushing their teeth.

"Hey," they greeted.

"You Browns out today?" asked Red. He meant the runners: our colour was Brown, then we each had a number to identify us. I was Brown 21. Reds were domestic, Blues hunters, Oranges cooks and Greens maintenance. We'd been allocated our colours and numbers when things had changed after the deaths of the Founders. My real name felt like a ghost: a faded reminder of the past. To my friends, I was Brown, the number only added if needed. In private, they called me Gonzales, after some cartoon mouse we had seen as kids, who could run really fast. The Boss didn't like the whole nickname thing though, so we kept it on the down-low. Still, it felt like a small way we could assert some form of personal identity, a way of refusing to become just another faceless Y. We called Myla the Boss as it reminded us just how dangerous she was: the title never let us forget that she was in charge.

"I think so," I answered. "We've been checking out the local hot spots for Saurian parties." I grinned and shot Red a sideways glance. His big goofy teeth shone back at me.

"Oh right," he said catching on. "So, you're going to be boogying with the big boys?"

I laughed at the gleam of delight in his eyes. He was stuck inside the school building most of his day, serving food, cleaning up. Unfortunately for him, he was often tasked with tidying the Boss' quarters, and he inevitably fell foul of her temper on a frequent basis. He'd once told me he'd give his right arm to have my job, to be given the freedom to leave Galex and roam. I suspected he wouldn't return given half the chance.

We all had a similar uniform: khaki trousers and black t-shirts. The aim was to dress us simply, and there was a ton of these outfits after a raid on a huge storeroom turned up enough of them to clothe a whole country. A band around our wrists gave our colour, making it easy for an X to see if we were doing what we were meant to.

We dressed and washed quickly. Our heads were kept shaved, so this saved time too. I think part of the idea was to make us easily distinguishable from the Xs – you could be safe in shooting a target with a shaved head. Even worse, I think it was easier to forget we were human too: if we all looked the same, we lacked any individuality. You could kill a Y and not really feel like you'd killed an actual person.

I joined Blue, Red and Orange at breakfast. We went through our usual jokey routine.

"The lumps in today's porridge are simply divine," drawled Red, smacking his lips.

"Superb," added Orange. "I must get the recipe to prepare similar fare for the Boss."

"You'd be strung up by your ankles if you even thought about serving her this muck," grumbled Blue, his stomach growling as he looked unhappily at his rations. The hunters tended to be the biggest and strongest Ys – there weren't many of them, and they were given the same rations as everyone else. The aim, I assumed, was to weaken them. If they were too physically powerful, they might cause more problems. The idea seemed to be to feed them just enough to do their job, but not enough to cause trouble. It was a bit like the way you might treat a dangerous dog.

"You out today, too, Blue?" I asked. He nodded. Hunters and runners often left Galex together and set off on the same path. The runners normally had to go further, leaving the hunters to stalk any prey they might come across. Last week, an abundance of rabbits had been brought back, so it was rabbit stew all round.

"Yup. Butch says he seen a couple of deer in the forests north west. We're gonna try and bring at least one of 'em back." His stomach rumbled noisily. "If it makes it that far! I might just have me a barbecue out beyond the wall." We chuckled, picturing him belching after a huge meal, picking his teeth with a leftover bone.

"I wish," I said.

*

Before

I can't remember much about my life before the world changed. I remember my mum. She had sparkly eyes and beautiful long raven hair that she kept in a thick plait. I remember playing. I remember laughter, other children, even friends. I remember safety, most of all.

Darkness came after. For a time, all was terror. The transformations. The destruction. Death stalked us, or so it felt – more than once my mum had to fight off a crazed X, desperate to kill any remaining Ys.

The Galex community gave us a sliver of hope when we pitched up, half-starved. Mum was welcomed and even I was tolerated. A Y, yes, but a child, a boy. Not a threat. Yet.

My mother died when I was six – nothing to do with the Epidemic, or Saurians, or anything. Cancer, they think. She got weaker and sicker, until she couldn't get out of bed. We made her as comfortable as we could. I held her hand until the end.

The next few years were overshadowed by the loss of my mother. I'm not saying they were bad, and they were definitely a lot better than the way things are now, but they were hard. There was a group of us kids without parents – we got used to being mollycoddled and fussed over by everyone and given pretty much free rein to do what we liked. Any fear of the Ys seemed to be receding as the fledgling community grew and healed.

Blue was my best friend growing up. We used to play-fight, run races, dig in the garden, whatever we could that meant being free outside. We bunked together in the main part of the school and despite my mum being gone, I didn't feel too lonely.

Of course, we played with Xs too, before the change came. Even then Cara stood out, with her wheat-coloured hair piled messily in a bun. She loved the outdoors too and had a knack for climbing trees higher than you would think possible. More than once she got out of trouble by hiding herself far above the heads of those looking for the culprits of some petty crime. She laughed easily and delightedly. You can't help but be drawn to someone like that, someone who reminds you of sunshine and warmth.

Her sister Myla was the opposite. Dark and brooding, her eyes flashed with malice. Whenever a Y was near, she would watch their every move and was quick to jump in if she saw any potential danger. Especially where Cara was involved. Any physical game – tag, dead man walking, even jump ropes –inevitably ended in a fight. It was clear Myla had a lot of pent-up aggression which she was only too happy to take out on the Ys.

And now she had power over us all.

When things changed, it literally happened overnight. The attack on the scientist. The Founders being killed. Suddenly, Ys were public enemy number one. As soon as the realisation hit that someone had mutated, we were herded together like cattle and locked into a few rooms. I remember being scared stiff, not having a clue what was going on. I remember that cold fear of having a gun trained on me, the click of the safety being taken off. Food was chucked in, as were buckets for toilets. You can imagine the stink after a few days. I honestly thought we were going to die, trapped like animals.

It might have been days or weeks. We lost all track of time, before we were eventually let out. However, things were never the same. Any freedom we had was gone. Xs were guarding us constantly, with weapons, and we were pushed around. They told us what had gone on, and to be fair we were all pretty scared ourselves. Nobody wants to become a hideous lizardy thing. It's certainly never been on top of my to-do list. Yet there seemed no answer as to why the two guys had transformed. It's a terrible thing, to be afraid of yourself, and what you could become. It means you never feel safe anywhere.

The tone of this new world was set very clearly when the basic rules were given whilst three armed guards pointed guns at our heads. We were tested to find out what our skills were – if we were physically fit, fast, decent cooks or good with our hands. Following that, we were renamed with colours and numbers. Our heads were shaved, uniforms doled out. Everything we thought about ourselves we were now told was wrong: we had a job to do, our purpose was to serve. We were lucky to be alive. We would do well to remember that. At any given time, Gloria could change her mind and kill us all. After what happened to the Founders, it was no more than we deserved.

I remember thinking: doesn't anyone ever consider what it feels like to be us? Don't they realise how scary it is, knowing you could transform into a monster at any time?

*

After

"Brown 21, reporting for duty."
The words that came out of my mouth every day we were called for. Runners didn't leave Galex every day – we were lucky and had time off to recuperate and recover. Before the Epidemic, people used to run a distance of around 26 miles

for fun. For fun! They were called marathons. To endure the pain and suffering that went with this kind of distance running was seen as a badge of honour. For us, 26 miles and sometimes more was all in a day's work. Some missions spanned several days, or even weeks, if the distances we needed to cover were far enough. Try running a marathon a day for a week and see if you can still stand up.

Blue sidled up. "Blue 13 reporting for duty!" He saluted and clapped his shoes together. I stifled a giggle. We had once watched an old movie where soldiers had done this whenever faced with someone of higher rank and shouted, "Sir, yes, Sir!" as loud as they could. We fell about, thinking how daft they were to do that when they didn't have to – they'd had a choice to serve, not like us. So now, every time he was called, Blue did this silly salute. It usually went unnoticed: except for a strange look, he got away with this mini rebellion. Today, though, he'd failed to notice Myla lurking in the background.

"What the hell is your problem, Blue 13?" She marched up to him and stared him down. At about a foot shorter than him, this also would have been funny, if it weren't for three nearby recruits with guns watching the whole thing.

"Apologies, Myla. Just excited for a day out hunting." Blue very carefully avoided all eye contact. For someone fairly cocky, this was unusual behaviour. I didn't blame him though – she was so volatile that if he eyeballed her back, she would probably order one of her minions to cut those eyeballs out. Sounds extreme, but we'd both seen her do worse.

Myla kept staring at him. "Good," she replied silkily,

"because I expect you to bring home the bacon. Because if you don't, we might have to look closer to home for what to chop up and eat for dinner." Blue looked uncomfortable but didn't flinch. I prayed that he had the sense to keep his mouth firmly shut. Luckily, he did. Also luckily, Myla seemed distracted because instead of tormenting him further she stalked away after dishing out brief instructions.

"You," her finger jabbed at the hunters. "South-west side. Bring back as much as you can carry, supplies are running low." She paired them off and sent others to different areas. She turned and pointed the same finger at me. "You. South-west too. About 22 miles. There're reports of a growing nest. I want you Ys out overnight, watching. Report back tomorrow. In fact," Myla paused and returned her focus to Blue. "You can stay the night too. Get these runners to help you carry back what you kill."

Blue knew better than to argue, having already raised his head above the parapet once. It would mean travelling further than hunters normally did, but at the same time, a night of freedom under the stars wasn't to be sniffed at. Me and Blue, plus Brown 6 and another Blue nicknamed Butch. We'd camp out, roast some of the catch – I was kind of looking forward to it.

"Yes, Myla," we mumbled, before grabbing our packs and preparing to leave.

"Oh, and before I forget," she added, a slight smile playing around her blood-red lips, "I'll be needing volunteers for a special mission coming up in the next few weeks. I trust I can rely on all of you. Especially you," she aimed at Blue.

We all stayed quiet but lowered our heads in assent.

Satisfied, she turned and headed back to her quarters. This must be the mission Cara had warned me against volunteering for, and if Myla wanted us to be a part of it as a way of punishing Blue for his little joke, I knew it must be bad.

*

Before

Imagine if at any point, for a reason unknown to you, you could change. Become someone else. Sound liberating? Make you feel powerful? Think again. The prospect of losing control, not knowing who you are anymore … or, worst of all, hurting someone you love … It doesn't bear thinking about.

But as a Y, I have to. Mutations are rare nowadays, but not impossible. My mother saw it happen to my dad. We were lucky to get away. Mum used to say she thought a part of my father was still in there, and that's why he allowed us to escape. I'm more of a realist. He was probably just disorientated, and this gave us a chance to get to safety. A few minutes more and we'd probably have been lunch. I'm just glad I can't remember anything about it.

In fact, I've only ever seen one mutation, and trust me, it was the most terrifying thing I've ever witnessed.

It happened on a run one day. There were four of us – we hadn't gone far. The rain was chucking it down, making the ground really squelchy with thick, gloopy mud. Blue and another hunter were there, and then me and Brown 9.

We always went in groups of three or more – the aim was that at least one of us would come back alive if anything happened. Today, though, visibility was poor, and we'd spent twenty minutes sheltering under a cracked, dried oak tree, desperately trying to stay dry whilst shivering in damp clothes.

"That's it, bruv, I am done," announced Blue. "No animal is stupid enough to be out in this, 'cept us. No point hanging around. I'm heading back."

The other hunter, who called himself Murdock after some crazy character from an old tv show called *The A Team*, seemed out of sorts. "Uh uh. No way I'm going back empty handed. I'm not facing the music because you're too lazy to hunt properly." The two hunters eyeballed each other.

"I'm. Not. Lazy," Blue intoned slowly and patronisingly, "it's PISSING it down! We've seen nothing moving, not even a toad looking for a puddle to splash about in. It's a waste of time, and if you can't see that, you're a dope." With that, he pushed Murdock away. "Now get out my face!"

That did it. Not known for his calm temper, Murdock launched himself at Blue with a roar. Me and Brown 9 stood aside, not wanting to get in the middle of these two – they were about twice our size, for starters. If one sat on us, we'd be crushed. Best let them work off their anger and then sort it out between themselves, we thought.

Unfortunately, that's not how things went. They grappled together on the ground for a bit, rolling about in the mud, shoving, slapping, punching. It wasn't the most sophisticated fight I'd ever seen – limbs went everywhere, partly because the sheets of rain made it difficult for them to see. Plus, the ground was slippery, so both kept tumbling, with legs akimbo. We could only tell them apart because Blue's dark brown skin contrasted to the pale white of Murdock.

"Shall we just head off and leave them to it?" Brown 9 was saying, when something changed.

Murdock suddenly stopped moving. He started groaning: a guttural sound which made the hairs on the back of your neck stand up and shiver. He was so still. Eerily still. Blue got up and backed away, unsure if this was a trick. As quickly as Murdock stopped moving, he began juddering and jerking uncontrollably. It looked like he'd stuck his fingers in a power socket and was being electrified. His face contorted, became rubbery. The pain must have been unbearable. His groans turned to shrieks.

We all started to back up. "What the f –" Blue stuttered, as Murdock started to disappear. Something was inside his body, and it was coming out. A scaly arm ripped through flesh, the rain sliding off a metallic-coloured claw. This claw then began scraping away the human skin, scratching away the body it was trapped in. In minutes, a full-grown reptile stood in front of us. A Saurian.

Open mouthed we stared, until one of us came to our senses.

"RUN!"

And we did. The rain pounded us. The ground sploshed as we ran through holes, puddles, sludge. A piercing howl shattered the air. I risked a glimpse behind me.

"It's chasing us!" I yelled, picking up my pace, spurred on by what I had seen. The muscular lizard was loping after us, its saliva-dripping jaws visible even in this weather.

My lungs felt like they were going to explode, my legs were pistons that I couldn't stop if I wanted to. Never had I been so scared. I had to be a machine and let adrenaline take over. My body surged forward: instinct took control. And, of course, fear. To think that two minutes ago, this creature had been my friend.

The horror didn't stop there. Next thing I knew, Brown 9 had slipped, crashing down to the ground. I paused to help him to his feet, but once up, he dropped down again, wincing in pain.

"My ankle. I think it might be broken." He tried to move it and gasped sharply.

"Here – lean on my shoulder – I'll support you," I offered desperately.

He smiled sadly. "There's no time." One glance showed the Saurian gaining steadily on us. "Go. No point two of us being dead. Go!" Without thinking about it further, I went. He was right. I could do nothing more for him.

That doesn't stop the nightmares though. In my dreams, I can still hear his screams. If I concentrate, I can even hear the moment his head is torn from his body. I try not to concentrate though – that's not a memory I want to relive.

We agreed not to tell the truth about what had happened to Murdock and Brown 9. We made up a story about them having vanished from camp overnight. We guessed they'd run away, we claimed. The Xs weren't too happy about it, but the fact that we had come back meant they didn't punish us too harshly. It was better than explaining about the mutation. Too many questions, that way. What had caused it? Had we come into contact with something that brought it on? No. Best if no one else knew. That way we didn't have to talk about it. Didn't have to think about what it meant. Didn't have to face the reality that anyone could transform at any time.

I can't forget though. I know this memory will forever be ingrained in my mind. The reason for the nightmares is not just the death of a friend, the horror of a full grown Saurian, it's not even the sounds I heard as it devoured 9's body. No. It's the guilt. Because part of me is glad it was 9 and not me. If I'm brutally honest, a deep-down part of me is glad he fell, because this gave me the chance to escape, while the creature was busy with him. If it hadn't been for his stumble, I would be dead.

And if I was dead, I would never have fallen in love with Cara.

FIVE

Even though it hurts, even though my knees feel every jolt, even though my lungs feel like they're being ripped to rags, there's something totally freeing about being a runner. With a steady pace, I'm in control. I can go where I want, look where I want, say what I want. Outside of Galex, I don't feel like just a number, I feel … whole again. The power in my legs spurs me on, further and further. Around me, the world looks magnificent: rolling hills, pathways that stretch as far as I can see, thickening forests dotting the horizon. The freedom is addictive: for a moment, I believe I can do anything, be anywhere. That endorphin rush kicks in, and for a moment, all the crap bits of life are left behind. If it weren't for Cara, and now the baby, I know in my heart that I would have started running by now and not stopped.

Today, though, we've put the brakes on. The hunters are not as used to long distances as we are, so we wanted to keep them in sight just in case we came across any issues. And by issues, I mean giant homicidal Saurians. We'd been sent out with a map drawn by the last set of runners who ventured this way, pointing to a potential nest towards the centre of a wooded area. Nests are often located in spaces like this – Saurians like shelter and they need a water source. They are natural hunters: patient, ruthless and without fear. The hope is that in this kind of environment we'll be able to watch them close up, whilst staying hidden. Another advantage we'll have is the cover of darkness, as they are much livelier at night, preferring to bask in the sun during the day, resting. Like snakes, I guess, they're cold-blooded and need sunlight to help them recharge their batteries.

6 and I were perfectly happy to jog rather than run. It meant a chance to actually take in the surroundings and even have a conversation, safe in the knowledge that no one was listening.

"I'm telling you," 6 said, "something's up."

"What do you mean?" I replied, dragging my mind back to the present moment, away from Cara and the baby.

"Something weird is going on," he repeated, sounding more urgent than he normally did. With black stubbly hair and a squint, 6 was definitely one of the more relaxed Ys. "There's planning afoot," he added mysteriously. He seemed genuinely worried.

For a terrifying moment I thought he knew about Cara and me. I was about to bluster some excuse when he expanded with: "The Boss. She's up to something."

I slowed my pace. "Up to something?" I questioned. Frowning, I realised she had been more visible recently. Watching, having hushed conversations with guards and recruits. Could 6 be right?

"I overheard a bit of a private meeting the other day," 6 continued. "I was out of sight, having been exercising near the training ground. I heard her say, 'We need them to volunteer, but obviously without giving them the whole story.' Do you think she meant us?"

I considered this. It seemed likely – Ys were being asked to volunteer, and it's doubtful that it was for something fun. More likely to be dangerous – Myla saw us as disposable anyway.

"It's not worth stressing about though," I argued. "We're put in danger all the time. We never have much choice in matters, if any. She's probably just thinking about a new mission where we have to go along and maybe get killed. Same old, same old."

To be honest, I thought, I've got bigger problems at the minute than worrying about what Myla will cook up for us next. It went without saying that she didn't care if we lived or died.

*

Before

It was crazy how different Myla and Cara were, even though they were sisters. One dark, the other fair, one cruel, the other kind. After we were reduced to the status of slaves, the treatment we got from Xs really varied, and the way they acted towards us gave you a sense of what kind of person they actually were. Myla, for instance, loved to hurt us. We were like pet dogs shivering in the corner as our volatile master kicked, punched or threw things at us for the tiniest offence. The rage she felt at the unfairness of life was directed squarely at us.

Cara, however, she was different. She treated us like human beings. If we passed her a glass, for instance, she would acknowledge our existence. If we crossed her path, she would make eye contact, even smile, and not simply plough forward, acting like we were invisible. It might sound small, but these things are important when you have absolutely no power.

It was about a year ago when things between us shifted. Myla had been in charge for about 15 months, and the quality of life for the Ys had already diminished. We lived in fear. She was so erratic, it wouldn't have been a surprise if she decided, on a whim, that every one of us should be shot. I remember reading about the Nazis in Germany from an old school textbook. I had a pretty good idea how the Jews must have felt.

Like I said, I was always drawn to Cara – her blonde hair and bright smile would light up a room. Her body during training moved so fluidly, I loved watching her fight, or work out. But it wasn't just physical – she was warm and always laughing. She took really good care of the younger recruits. I think, to a degree, she even toned down her sister's worse impulses. God only knows how bad Myla'd be if it weren't for Cara being around.

As part of the training for the X recruits, a night was spent outside the wall. The thinking was to see if they could protect themselves, and to see how they coped away from the safety of the city. It was telling to see how some were naturally brave whilst others just went to pieces. The idea was to hunt down and kill a Saurian – a bit like a rite of passage. It was dangerous, but to protect the city, these girls had to face it. They usually sent about six recruits, a runner, and of course, Cara.

This particular trip was the first I'd been sent on, and to be honest, I wasn't thrilled about the prospect. It felt like I'd be Billy No-Mates, stuck on my own with a bunch of people trying to prove how tough they were. I could see the runner becoming a bit of a punch bag, and I'm sure Myla actively encouraged this mentality. I hadn't counted on Cara, though. First thing she said was, "Recruits, part of this expedition is about learning respect. Respect for the chain of command, respect for each other. Respect for the Saurians –" At this, the tallest recruit scoffed.

"That's right, Becka, respect," Cara repeated, eyebrow raised as she looked unamused. Chastened, Becka dropped her gaze to the floor. This wasn't done out of fear, I realised, but out of respect. This is what made Cara different from Myla: she earned respect, rather than commanding it. It's what would make her a better leader, it dawned on me.

Cara continued. "I also expect respect to be shown to –" at this, she paused, turning to me. I was so surprised to be included in the conversation that it took me a minute to realise she wanted to know my name.

"Er – Brown 21, Sir. I mean, Protector." She tried to hide a smile, but the side of her face still dimpled. I could feel the blush rising to my whole face – what a moron! She must think I was a bumbling idiot who could barely string a sentence together!

"Brown 21 here is part of our team for this expedition, and you will treat him as such. Any offhand behaviour, any violence –" her eye caught Becka's, who simply nodded to show she understood, "and you'll be sent back having failed. Clear?"

"Clear, Protector!" The recruits sounded in unison.

"Excellent. Well, time is ticking and we've got a way to travel before sunset, so grab your stuff and let's head out." They scampered off to collect their bags. Without a hunter, we took rations with us, along with tents, weapons and other essentials. It meant a rucksack each.

"Let me know if any of them ignores what I just said," Cara told me, before picking up her own bag. "Part of this experience will show who follows orders and who doesn't. We need recruits who will work as a team and listen to the chain of command, otherwise they're not suited to the job."

"Okay, sure," I replied, my mouth dry and voice cracked from lack of use. It felt very confusing, an X talking to me like I was an equal. A human being. It hadn't happened in a very long time.

"Oh, and by the way," she added, a cheeky grin playing on her lips, "I remember a time when I was the champion tree climber. Don't think you can out-climb me on this trip either!"

And with that, she marched off to join the recruits. Butterflies rose in my stomach – she remembered me from before! This told me a couple of things. One, she'd noticed me, perhaps in the way I'd noticed her and two, she wasn't following the Galex rules of ignoring Ys unless absolutely necessary. I picked up my own backpack and swung it on my shoulder, a ray of hope rising that if she could break this rule, she might be prepared to break others.

*

After

It was about 4 o'clock when we got to our destination, and the light was slowly starting to dip. The woods looked beautiful; orange leaves were starting to fall and coat the ground with bronze. Further out of the cities, nature had recovered much more quickly, and the forested areas were thickening as trees fought to grow closer to the sun. This was great for our purposes, and we set up camp in a small clearing surrounded by dense bushes.

By the time we'd got a fire going, the two hunters arrived looking weary, and slumped to the ground.

Blue groaned. "How you guys run so far in a day is beyond me," he complained, kicking off his shoes to rub his feet. "My feet are killing me! I must have, like, twenty blisters."

Butch nodded, "Same, man. My legs feel like they're on fire as well."

"You get used to it," 6 chipped in. "You'll feel it worse tomorrow though," he added chirpily. "Something about a delayed muscle reaction. You'll probably struggle to even stand up!"

"Oh, great," muttered Blue. He stretched his back. "The journey home'll be fun then. Mind you, I could just stay here. Set up a little camp, eat and sleep to my heart's content."

"Until a Saurian comes along and makes you his breakfast," I told him, grinning.

"Oh, you have so little faith in my survival skills! I'd run rings round those tools." We all chuckled, picturing Blue single-handedly bringing down a pack of Saurians.

Blue opened his pack and pulled out three dead rabbits. "Ta da! And for my next trick … roasted rabbit!" He chucked one to Butch and they set about skinning the poor creatures. My stomach growled: a meaty feast would be much appreciated.

Minutes later, and the rabbits were slowly cooking over the fire. Carefully, 6 and I found the local water source and refilled our canteens. We knew we had to keep our wits about us with a nest nearby, but the only sign of life was a couple of deer grazing by the stream. I suspected that if Blue caught sight of them, their days would be numbered.

"Any sign of them?" Butch asked when we returned, the smell of the rabbit making my mouth water.

"Not really," I answered. "A couple of tracks in the muck by the stream. They must be sleeping somewhere quiet before a night of fun and games."

"Have you got a plan? Normally us hunters are safely home by now, leaving you runners to do the dangerous jobs. Do you just hang about and see what happens?"

"There's a bit more to it than that," I laughed. "We tend to get fed and watered, rest up for a few hours and then when night falls, find somewhere near the water source to hide, and spread ourselves out. Hollowed out logs, thick bushes, even up trees all work well. We cover ourselves in mud to hide any scent, although to be honest, Saurians don't seem the brightest of creatures. They appear to hunt based on sights and sounds, rather than smell. We then just make a note of anything we observe. Come morning, when the Saurians go back to sleep, we head off, stopping for a cat nap a bit further away." Explaining it like this made it seem a bit risky, being so close to the beasts.

Blue obviously thought so too. "Don't they ever see you? Do you have to stay totally still all night?" He frowned. Blue was a fidgeter: he could barely sit still for five minutes, let alone a whole night.

"We've been lucky so far. Some runners don't make it back to Galex, so who knows? The Saurians tend to move around a fair bit at night, so they shouldn't be close to you for too long. Just be careful when they're near your hiding spot."

Blue grunted, clearly still a bit wary. Changing the subject, Butch said, "Food should be done."

We ate well. The rabbit was delicious, and full bellies made us all feel more reassured about the night ahead. After dinner we took it in turns to snooze for an hour or so, hoping to feel recharged. Blue and I were on first watch, and sat staring into the fire, listening to the crackles and pops as it burnt.

"Do you really think them missing runners ended up on the Saurian menu?" he asked, after a period of silence.

I shrugged. "It's a definite possibility. Where else could they be?"

Lying on his side, Blue repositioned himself to face me. "Escaped?" His tone became hushed, excited. "I bin hearing things for a while now. There's a city, far south of us in

Galex. It's called Amex. Rumour is, they do things differently there." His eyes were wide and shining, the whites standing out like pearls against his mahogany skin.

"What do you mean, differently?" His excitement had made me more alert.

"More equal. Ys and Xs. Like how things used to be. And," he paused. Blue loved to add a dramatic edge to his storytelling. "Apparently they have a cure. Or at least, they're damned close to one."

He folded his hands, as if to say, see? You can't argue with that.

"How'd you know this?" I asked sceptically. Surely if a place like this existed, we'd all be queuing up to go live there.

Blue shuffled closer again, after glancing at 6 and Butch, to check they were asleep.

"I heard it from Red 16, that weird hairy dude who used to bunk next to me. He went by the name Chewbacca. Remember?"

I nodded. He'd snored like a pig and thankfully was moved out of our dorm.

"He used to bunk with two runners. They told him about it – they'd heard about Amex out on one of their missions, heard it from a couple of Ys they met. He reckons they nearly went off with them there and then, it sounded so great. But they came back – thinking of the greater good, you see," he tapped his nose, knowingly.

"The greater good?"

"See, by coming back, they hoped to save ALL the Ys. Find a way to get us all there." Something sparked in my mind.

"Was this when Gloria was in charge?" I questioned.

"Yup," he nodded. "Don't you remember that mission she went on? When she was killed? By Ys?" he added, his tone sounding disbelieving.

"I do remember," I said. "It was really weird –"

Properly excited, now, Blue butted in "Yes! It was pretty much brushed under the carpet. I mean, why didn't the Boss torture us, really make us suffer? You know she loves that," he spat disgustedly on the ground.

"Thinking about it, you're right. There wasn't much of a fuss made at all. It was just like, Gloria's dead, now Myla's in charge," I added thoughtfully.

"Exactly. And you know, Gloria was always tight with Cara – wasn't she being lined up to take over? Plus, another thing," Blue was really warming to his conspiracy theory, "the Ys who they reckon killed her. Think about it. Why would they? They were going to Amex, a place where they would be treated equally! It makes no sense."

"So, you think Myla sent someone on that mission to kill all three of them? Get Gloria out the way and frame the Ys, killing them too so they couldn't claim their innocence?" As I said the words aloud, it all clicked into place. It did make sense.

"You've got it!" He slapped his thigh in emphasis. "It's clever when you think about it. Get a lackey to do your dirty work. Take over the world. Kill same lackey to get rid of any witnesses and –"

"You have Galex. The lackey – who was she?"

"Amina, I think she was called? Always in Myla's pocket. Another nasty piece of work."

I vaguely remembered her – she was hailed as some sort

of hero for bringing Gloria's murderers to justice. I think she left, though, or at least she wasn't in the city anymore.

"You think she was killed too?" I questioned.

"For sure," Blue affirmed confidently. "Fits Myla's M.O. to a tee."

I sat up, looking intensely into the flames. It was certainly a compelling story – whether it was more than that, I didn't know. If it was true though, it meant that Myla had robbed her sister of power. It meant she'd also indirectly robbed us Ys of a shot at freedom.

"But anyway," Blue continued, "those Ys who got killed – they used to bunk with Chewbacca. They told him about Amex – said it was really hush hush, couldn't let it get out, and all that. Didn't want anyone's hopes to get too high."

"Why did they tell him, then?" I pondered.

Blue shrugged, yawning. "I dunno, wondered that myself. Maybe they had a bad feeling that things wouldn't go the way they hoped? P'rhaps they wanted someone to know about Amex, in case anything happened to them. Sort of like a security policy."

I nodded. It seemed a reasonable suggestion.

"So," Blue carried on, sitting up next to me so close I could feel his breath on my cheek. "Shall we ditch these two early tomorrow? Just go? I reckon we'd have a fair chance of finding the place. And what've we got to lose?"

My heart sank. I couldn't. How could I abandon Cara now? And the baby?

I sighed. "Nice thought, bruv," I said thinking quickly, "but maybe we should plan for this? Next mission together we could take extra supplies, maybe find Chewbacca again and get more information. Seems a bit of a risk just legging it tonight." I looked at him, holding my breath in the hope that he bought it.

Blue flopped back again. "Whatever, man," he answered finally. "Just don't know how much more I can take."

He turned his back to me. With Butch and 6 stirring, I lay down too, feeling guilty at having to disappoint my friend.

SIX

Someone shook me roughly awake. 6 stood over me. "It's time," he said.

I jumped up and rolled my bed mat up, stuffing it into my backpack. Butch was stamping on the fire, and Blue stretched his arms until they cracked. The sun was so low now only a red glow misted the surroundings.

"I'm shattered," complained Blue. "We really have to stay awake all night? This is some kind of torture, man!"

"Yep," answered 6 briskly, "but it's nothing compared to being eaten alive by a Saurian." He gathered up his bag ready to leave.

"Sorry, my bad," grumbled Blue. I shot him a glance intended to say, he's always a bit grumpy without sleep, but Blue was avoiding my eyes.

We'd scouted out some hiding spots earlier in the day. We probably had about an hour before the Saurians were up and about at full capacity, so we needed to get moving and be in position as soon as possible. I was up a tree, as usual:

Saurians didn't like to climb, so I knew I'd be pretty safe. 6 was up high too, as he was spry and little. The Blues were bigger and heavier, so we found them places on the ground.

We said our quick goodbyes and agreed to meet up the following morning when the sun had reached above the tree line. Blue still wouldn't look at me. I resolved to tell him the truth about Cara on the journey home – I couldn't let this go on, with him thinking I was letting him down. He deserved to know the real reason I couldn't just abandon our lives in Galex.

I grabbed the lower branches of my chosen tree. Oak. This meant strength. I clasped the next branch and clambered up rapidly – years of practice meant I was a dab hand at this. I smiled, remembering how, as a kid, Cara would skin both knees in her haste to climb, just to make sure she got the highest. Things hadn't changed. Reaching a hefty looking branch about 15 feet above the ground, I wedged my backside against the trunk and dug in.

*

Before

That first trip with Cara and the recruits feels like a dream now, but it changed everything for me. For us. It started out as I'd expected – the Xs all hung out together and I was pretty much ignored. Cara's focus was on their training: teaching them how to hunt and fish, survival skills and team building. It was a long day of activity followed by setting up camp, which for these recruits seemed to be a major mission.

I had to bite my tongue as the one called Tyra was paired with Becka, and they took about two hours to put a tent up. They'd not banged the tent pegs in hard enough though, so they'd only been inside it five minutes when the whole thing collapsed onto their heads. They dissolved into fits of giggles and finally, with a sigh of exasperation, Cara showed them how it was done.

"I was hoping you'd show enough initiative to put it up yourselves!" she joked.

"Aw, we knew you'd help out if we looked pathetic enough," Tyra retorted, her cheeky grin giving her away.

The evening was spent preparing the food caught earlier, and songs around the fire. The girls were surprisingly good, and they even performed dance routines they'd seen from old music videos. I sat a bit separate, and they pretty much left me to my own devices, which suited me fine. I actually enjoyed it: the open air, the crackling of a fire, and Cara.

Her facial features accentuated by the glimmering flames, she looked more beautiful than ever. The light played on her golden hair, and made her green eyes shine like emeralds. She was so good with the recruits – kind, encouraging, but firm when needed. They clearly loved her – I could see why.

I made my excuses, and disappeared early to my tent, quite honestly glad to have a bit of time to myself – not something you get a lot of living in a dorm. A noise, or movement outside of the tent woke me after what I guessed was a couple of hours. I stuck my head out of the tent door, and marvelled at the brightness of a full moon. The fire was still smouldering, glowing embers still burning. Poking at it with a stick was Cara. She saw me emerge and beckoned me over.

"Couldn't sleep either?"

I shook my head and perched on the end of the log next to hers.

"I've sent those on watch to bed, no point a whole load of us missing out on sleep. They'll need it for tomorrow, anyway. Want a hot drink? I'm trying to get this fire going again to boil some water." She jabbed the stick at a blackened lump.

"Let me," I offered. She passed me the stick. I got up, grabbed some dried grass and crumbled it onto the embers, blowing gently as I twisted the stick. Soon, a pretty decent fire had taken hold.

"Nice skills!" Cara said admiringly. "Not just a pretty face, hey?" I look sharply at her, to see if she was making fun of me. With my shaved head, I thought my blue eyes popped out, and my nose looked too prominent. She smiled warmly back at me. "Not good with compliments, I see?"

"Can't say I get too many," I answered, my voice sounding cracked, my throat dry.

She sighed. "No, I guess not." She rubbed her hands together, warming them in front of the flames. "Not all Xs are like my sister, you know," she continued, looking sideways at me. "Some of us really want a better society, where we can all live together. People are scared is all, you know …" she trailed off, obviously not sure how to say, 'we're scared you might transform into a scaly, human-eating lizard.'

"So are we," I replied. "Also, not all monsters look like Saurians." This was risky. I was basically suggesting her sister was a monster. It was a bold move – but I had to know where she stood.

She sighed again. "I guess you're right. Although monstrous behaviour doesn't always mean a monster – sometimes it comes from fear and hurt and anger."

I nodded, acknowledging this defence of Myla, even if it was of no real difference to those she persecuted. We sat in silence until the water in front of us began to bubble.

Once we had our drinks to blow on and sip, conversation flowed a little easier. Time passed, we chatted, and for a time we forgot where we were, what we were doing, who we each were. We simply enjoyed each other's company. It felt easy. We could make each other laugh; we could share private emotions. The sun started to creep up behind us, but we hardly noticed. Only when the recruits started unzipping their tents in the early hours did we busy ourselves in the camp, so it looked like I'd just got up early and Cara'd set me to work helping out. She kept glancing at me though – and I kept glancing back. Whenever we made eye contact, grins spread across our faces.

The journey back was fairly uneventful. Cara kept pace with the recruits, and I lagged behind, still lost in the memory of the previous night. It wasn't until we were nearly back at Galex that Cara slowed, letting the others go on ahead.

"Say I wanted to keep talking," she said shyly, "can you think of a way that would be possible?"

Inwardly my heart leapt. Despite the dangers for her and definitely for me, I couldn't bear the thought of not seeing and talking to her again.

"Well, there's always future expeditions. You'll need a

reliable runner. But also, if you need to talk before, there's a garden outside my dorm window. It used to be part of the kitchen –"

"I know it," she interrupted. "Tall sweet peas and roses at the back."

"That's it! Well, there's quite a few hidden nooks and crannies there for a private chat. If I were needed, say in the middle of the night, someone would just need to throw a handful of pebbles at the dorm window on the far left-hand side. Luckily, I'm a light sleeper." We smiled at each other. My stomach felt like it was doing back-flips.

"Great! Well, I'll bear that in mind." And with that, she winked at me and sprinted off to catch up with the recruits.

*

After

Hoots. Squeaks. Flaps. Chirps. Despite the dark, the forest was busy. Life teemed around me, and I was grateful: not much was going on. I'd been up the oak tree for hours; it was all I could do not to fall asleep. My eyes kept shutting, my head lolling, until it dropped and I snapped awake. What I wouldn't give for a comfy bed!

The moon was bright, casting a glow across the canopy of the forest. I could see squirrels, badgers, bats – all collecting food as they moved quietly below. A sudden movement caught my attention. A Saurian pouncing. Something shrieked as the creature gobbled it down, bones cracking in its teeth.

I'd seen them close up before, but I was always amazed by the texture and size of them. They were almost silver in this light and shimmered like a fish out of water. To think, they were part of my genetic code. I shuddered.

Keeping very still, I watched the Saurian. It wasn't alone. Emerging from behind the trees were two more. They communicated to each other with a series of clicks and hisses – this was new to me. I knew they lived in nests but hadn't thought about them talking to each other.

They stopped still for a moment, their communication continuing. Was this development of language new? Was this why we'd been sent out – to see if they were evolving?

From my vantage point, I could see much more than I would have been able to at ground level. As I watched, I saw the three beasts set up a kind of formation – not that dissimilar to one we might use in a game of football to try and make sure no one on the opposing team could sneak by us. This form of triangle allowed them to move forward, still clicking to each other to let them know exactly where they were, until they had something in a bush surrounded.

Too late I realised what the something was. A cry from the bush told me it was Blue. Realising he was trapped, he made a desperate break for freedom, roaring as he lunged out, rapidly building up to a sprint. My heart was in my mouth. A strangled noise escaped: I clamped my hand over my lips. My chest felt like it might explode. No matter what, I had to stay silent – even two of us would have no chance against three large Saurians.

Despite Blue's speed, he didn't make it far. The Saurians rounded on him, again working together as they chased and tackled him to the ground. The moonlight caught the whites of his eyes for a second, letting me see the terror in his expression. My heart lurched; I bit down on my knuckles to prevent a cry escaping up.

From then on, it was quick. The biggest of them slashed with his claws, ripping down Blue's back. It felt like someone had punched me in the stomach, so powerful was my reaction to witnessing this. My friend, alone. He wasn't moving. As if to make sure he was dead, the enormous beast raised the other arm and swiped again. There was no doubt left in my mind that Blue was gone.

Tears streamed silently down my face as I rocked back and forth, desperately trying to calm down. Blue was gone; I couldn't help him now. We all knew the risks of missions like this. There was no point me getting involved – it would be suicide. This rational thinking didn't stop me from feeling like a terrible friend though.

Crowding around the body, the Saurians communicated again, before dragging Blue away by the feet. The forest went quiet. The presence of these enemies had scared away all other wildlife, at least for the time being. All I could picture was Blue running and then … It played over and over, like a film in my head. I couldn't remember where Butch and 6 were – had they seen? Were they safe? I felt completely powerless: I knew I couldn't leave the safety of my tree, particularly with those three Saurians nearby. I'd never felt so lonely in my life.

It was going to be a long night.

*

Before

It was around two weeks after the mission with Cara, when a shower of taps woke me one night. I lay still, listening to the varying breaths and snores and murmurs coming from the beds around me. There it was again. I stole out of bed and, staying as quiet as I could, tiptoed to the window. Cracking the blinds, I caught sight of a shadow ducking behind the trellis at the back of the garden. Smiling to myself, I dressed quickly, my heart already pumping at twice its normal speed. Blue cracked one eye open – I simply put a finger to my lips and crept out.

When I reached the garden, she was sitting on the little bench right in the corner, her long hair curled over her left shoulder in a loose ponytail. It was the perfect spot to stay hidden in the shadows, with blossoming fruit trees for added camouflage.

"Hi," I said brightly, trying not to show just how excited I was to see her.

"Hi back," she whispered, patting the bench, gesturing me to sit. I obeyed.

"Couldn't sleep again. Thought I'd see how you were keeping and to tell you I remembered something. From when we were little."

I grinned. I'd been thinking back to those times as well, letting a few memories resurface from the haze of childhood. The fact that she'd obviously been thinking about me too made me feel fuzzy.

"I must have been about seven, so I'd guess you were eight. It was one of our epic Hide and Seek games. You know, the ones that lasted a whole afternoon and usually ended in everyone giving up, except for Myla? She'd get so annoyed when she finally came out from her hiding place, and we'd all been playing tag or sunbathing for about two hours."

I chuckled, nodding. Myla would come stomping out, wearing a murderous frown, demanding to know why we had stopped the game before she'd been crowned the victor.

"She never could face losing." Cara's tone had changed. She sounded weary. "Anyway," she brightened. "On this day, I remember finding an amazing tree for climbing – thick branches, lots of foliage, and so high! I clambered up, so pleased with myself, then bam! I landed on your lap!"

I laughed aloud. "I remember! I thought I'd found the perfect, comfortable spot to hide in and suddenly this little person jumps on me!"

"I was so mad! I think I said something like, *who do you think you are, stealing my tree!*"

"That's it, exactly! I couldn't believe it! I thought, that's so cheeky, I was here first! That didn't stop you though, you simply got me to give you a leg up and you climbed even higher!"

She giggled. "I figured that even if they found you, they'd never think of looking any higher."

"But you didn't count on me grassing you up," I confessed, with a sidelong glance at her.

"You didn't!"

"Guilty," I said, holding up my hands.

It was amazing how at ease I felt. Usually when talking to an X, I was on guard, watching what I said. You got to learn the hard way that there were consequences for an ill-advised comment.

We stayed several hours. We didn't see another soul – the guards didn't tend to patrol the garden, so we had total privacy. After this, she'd come every week or so. It got so I looked forward to it for days, and if I woke up in the morning without having had a midnight visit, my heart sank.

Blue guessed something was going on, and he got fairly close to the truth, teasing me about a crush on an X. It was dangerous though, of course – I'm sure that's why he only ever mentioned it to me in private. If he'd have known it was Cara, he'd have realised just how high the stakes were.

*

After

After witnessing the attack on Blue, I didn't sleep a wink, despite not seeing hide nor hair of any other Saurians all night. When dawn finally rose, I must've replayed Blue's death a million times over in my head. Could I have helped? Should I have helped? The guilt gnawed at my insides, made worse by the fact that we hadn't really been speaking right before he'd died.

Shifting my legs, I realised that every part of me ached, a combination of yesterday's run and staying in the same position for most of the night. I slowly and wearily shuffled down the tree, landing with a thud. I felt like I'd done ten rounds in a boxing ring: everything hurt. Carefully, I limped back to the clearing, our meeting point. 6 was already there, plonked down on a log, staring at the ashes of yesterday's fire.

He looked up at me, his eyes haunted.

"You saw?" I asked him, sitting heavily next to him.

"Not all of it," he replied. "I heard him shriek and saw him try to run but they chased him down." His grey eyes turned to mine. "I've never seen Saurians act like that before."

"I know, me neither," I agreed. "It's like they were organised."

"That's it! I swear they planned it. They knew where Butch was and –"

"Hold up," I interrupted. "Butch? Don't you mean Blue 13?"

For a minute, 6 looked confused. "Tall and white? That's Butch isn't it?"

It was, no question. Blue was black and stocky. But this meant –

"They attacked both of them!" I realised, horrified.

"Seriously? You saw a different attack?"

"Must've. I heard them talking to each other, with clicks and hisses, then – they worked as a team to trap him. I felt so helpless," I admitted.

"Same, bro," muttered 6. "I felt like such a coward sitting up in a tree. But I couldn't get my legs to even move."

I stood up. "We've got to head back as fast as we can. I don't think I could sleep after what I've just seen anyway." 6 shook his head in agreement that sleeping was off the menu. "We've got to warn everyone – the Saurians are clearly evolving, and if that continues, we could be in serious trouble."

"Too right. I don't even want to think about what happens if they get in the city walls."

We ate some of our rations for energy and silently packed everything up. No matter how tired we felt, I knew we'd keep a steady brisk pace, lost in our own thoughts. With each pounding step, the name Cara rang through my head. The ordeal reminded me just how important it was to protect her and the baby.

SEVEN

"So, the Saurians are planning things now?" Myla's voice dripped with sarcasm. "They've gone from mindless beasts to intelligent beings, what, overnight?"

6 and I stood in front of her and the recruits, feeling like a couple of naughty schoolboys. The run back had been a solemn one; we'd barely said two words to each other, except to agree the details of what we'd say when we got back.

"We can only tell you what we saw," I replied, bristling inside but trying to keep my voice neutral.

"Well, tell us again then. So, they started talking and then ganged up on your friends and ripped them apart." The casual way she spoke about Blue's fate made me wince.

"Are you sure they weren't just loping along and came across him? From what I remember he was rather big, and he had a big mouth too," Myla said disdainfully. "Perhaps he was poorly hidden. It wouldn't take much intelligence to spot a pair of enormous feet sticking out from a bush and put two and two together to find a tasty snack." She turned her head towards the recruits behind her and rolled her eyes. They snickered dutifully. Cara stood to the left of her sister, her face sober. Her eyes sought mine, however, and I could see the sympathy in them.

"I can assure you, Blue was well disguised," I answered, tears stinging my eyes at how cruel she could be. I was determined not to let her see she'd got to me, so I fought to keep the waver out of my voice. "I didn't say speaking, I said communicating. It might be a fairly undeveloped code they have, the basics of a language, maybe. But I can tell you with certainty that they worked as a pack and hunted him out. Brown 6 saw them do similar with Butch. I mean, Blue 22. I don't think that's a coincidence."

"Maybe not," Myla admitted. "However, at this stage, I can't see we have too much to be concerned about. They're hardly reading poetry and debating life's big questions. I think we'll be safe enough for the time being." She made as if to dismiss us.

"We're sorry about your friends," Cara spoke softly, but still earned a sharp look from Myla.

"Better them than us," she retorted, staring down her nose at us. "Two less potential mutations, and some interesting intel. A successful mission, I'd say."

I could practically feel 6's blood boil next to me. The way she spoke about us! Cara's face was inflamed; I knew she felt the slight nearly as much as I did.

"Let's get out of here, before we say something we'll regret," I muttered quietly to 6. Grudgingly, he nodded, and we turned to go.

Just as we pulled the door open, Myla called, "Oh, by the

way. A new mission is coming up in a few weeks' time. We'll need a fair number of Ys to take part. I trust I can rely on you two to lead and recruit others?" Cara's eyes widened; she looked stricken. The tiniest shake of her head.

"Sure," I answered, shrugging, before turning and walking out. The humiliation from the debriefing had burned me – perhaps I wanted to show her that I wasn't completely powerless. I could still make my own decisions, even if it meant putting myself in danger.

*

Before

The late-night meetings between me and Cara continued for several months. For days after we'd spoken, I'd feel like I was floating on air, my stomach churning with excitement. I knew more about Cara than anyone, and in return I'd really opened up to her. Hopes, dreams, fears, fantasies – nothing was off limits.

It was when I was telling her about my mother that Cara took things a step further.

"I'll never forget her final moments," I shared, having just told her about the cancer and how tiny Mum had looked in her hospital-style bed at the end. "I held onto her hand, dry as paper. I could feel every bone and sinew and vein. Yet, she was still warm and comforting, life still pulsed through her. It hit me then, that she'd be gone before the day was over and I'd never get to see or touch her again." Cara placed her hand over mine. The touch of her skin brought the memory back even more vividly, and tears started to trickle down my cheeks. "I've never felt as scared as I did in that moment. Not even when faced with a nest of Saurians." I smiled weakly. "The world felt empty, like I was going to have to navigate it alone. I still miss her every day."

"I know how you feel," said Cara. "Losing my mum was one of the worst things to ever happen to me. Seeing her broken body … something broke in me, too." Now she was the one to wipe away a tear. "I'm not sure I'll ever be fully 'fixed' again." She smiled wanly.

I squeezed her hand back. "I don't think you're broken," I said. "If anything, you're stronger than you were, because you've had to be. I suppose it's more like a scar you carry with you. It will always be a part of you: you'll never forget what happened, but you'll keep growing in spite of it."

Cara stared at me.

"How did you get to be so wise?" she asked admiringly.

"Just raw talent, I think." I grinned. She moved closer. Our lips touched, and a thousand tiny explosions went off inside of me. This is what love feels like, I thought to myself.

*

After

She is just a class A bitch," 6 fumed. He was pacing up and down the dormitory, seething with rage following Myla's treatment of us both. "How can she just not care? People died!" His voice cracked.

"I'm not sure she sees us as people," I suggested. "More

like commodities. Things she can use."

"God only knows what this mission will involve. You goin' ahead with it?" He looked at me askance, his eyes betraying his fear.

I resolved myself. "Yes. Whatever it is, it's got to be better than sitting around here helpless all day." The image of Blue's last moments flashed through my head again. I blinked them away.

"Have you ever thought about it? How it happens? The mutations?" His voice hushed, 6 came and sat close to me, his left eye twitching with anxiety. Even a conversation about this could put us in extreme danger. "Have you ever thought what causes them?"

"Of course," I answered honestly. Surely every Y had. I clung to the possibility that some of us were immune – a horrible death from a disease seemed preferable to becoming a beast. Especially as that meant you would have no problem killing the people you cared about.

My last conversation with Blue popped back into my mind. At the time, I'd dismissed the rumour about Amex as a myth. Could such a place exist?

"Every time I feel anything – a sniffle, a cough, a sore throat – I'm terrified I've caught the virus. Sometimes I wish it would happen – just so as I could stop worrying about it." 6 glanced at me, checking I wasn't judging him too harshly.

"I can't think about it," I responded truthfully. "I think if I did, I'd go mad."

In my darker moments I had gone there. It was like having the Sword of Damocles dangling above you: a sword suspended by a single hair, waiting to fall and slice you up at any moment. "I have to live for the moment, take each day is it comes. *Carpe diem*, they used to call it. Seize the day."

6 nodded thoughtfully. I could tell he understood, but the twitch in his eye remained, suggesting he wasn't going to stop worrying about it any time soon.

I decided to take a risk. "Have you ever heard any talk about another city? One that's close to a cure?"

I could practically see the cogs turning in his brain as he processed what I'd said.

"No … but I remember two bunk mates whispering really furtively once in the middle of the night. I only caught bits of the conversation, odd words like travel, disease, south. They disappeared from the kitchens soon after, do you remember? Their bodies were discovered just outside the city."

I did remember. There was some story about them being traitors, stealing supplies. I'd always thought it was strange that their corpses were found on the other side of the wall.

Understanding seemed to dawn on 6's face. "Why? Do you know something?" A tiny glimmer of hope and excitement rippled across his expression, bringing a light to his grey eyes which I realised had been absent since we returned from the mission.

"Not really," I said hastily, keen not to let him get carried away when I had no idea if this place was anything more than a made-up story. "Just something Blue said. I wondered if it was possible."

6 thought hard. "If anyone were to know, I reckon it'd be Brown 1. He was the first runner, and he's been out on more missions than the rest of us put together. I partnered with

him once, and he knew the land like the back of his hand. And not just the land surrounding Galex – I'm talking miles and miles. You could speak to him?"

I must've looked blank. "Oh, you probably haven't met him," he added. "He doesn't go out anymore. He got attacked the last mission he went on – lost a leg. Came back with deep gashes across his body, too. Not sure he's fully recovered," 6 said, tapping the side of his head to show me what he meant. "He tends to stay in the old library. Just sits there for hours on his own. He doesn't say much anymore, but it might be worth a try. If anyone's heard of it, it'll be him."

*

Before

Things between Cara and me had been moving so slowly, it suddenly felt like we were moving at a 100 miles an hour after that first kiss. Not that I minded. Like I said, this was love. I just worried about the future – and by that, I mean I couldn't see one that featured both of us in it, together. We could only meet in secret and there would be serious consequences for both of us if anyone found out what was going on. Blue kept up his teasing of me having a thing with an X, but I never revealed the full truth of who I was seeing to him. It wasn't that I thought he'd betray me – I trusted him with my life. I just didn't want to place him in any danger, so figured the less he knew, the better. If Myla found out, though? Both our lives would be over.

It wasn't until another expedition around ten months

later that we had chance to get more physical. The next batch of recruits were getting close to graduating, so a mission was arranged to put them through their final paces. Cara asked for me directly – her excuse was that I kept my distance and didn't speak unless I was spoken to! This was the ideal Y in Myla's eyes.

Out on the expedition, it was similar to the last one: a talk about respect, me keeping my distance and going to bed early. Only this time, we'd already agreed that Cara would wait until she was sure the recruits were fast asleep, with those on patrol at the far end of the camp, before sneaking into my tent.

I'm not going to paint you a picture or give away too many details. Needless to say, it was probably the best night of my life. I'm pretty sure Cara enjoyed herself too. It was a killer when dawn broke, and she had to head back to her own tent, so as not to arouse suspicion. I can't even imagine what would have happened if the recruits had realised what was going on. Luckily, they were too wrapped up in their own experiences to think about me.

She left me that night with a kiss, whispering, "I love you." It was the first time she'd told me that. I kissed her back.

"I love you too, always will."

*

After

The library was a neglected corner of the school, located right in the far top-left corner of the main building up several flights of stairs. Nobody really went up there anymore and when I pushed open the heavy door, it creaked from too little usage. The room was filled with tall shelves, piled high with a cornucopia of books. Hard backed, colourful, they lined the walls like gems of light. Cobwebs hung low and the musty air swirled with dust.

"Hello?" I called.

A rustle sounded from up a short staircase to a mezzanine level, also rammed full of books. A head popped up from above a tall pile. Brown 1 was thin, with longer hair than the rest of us – I guess if he'd been forgotten about, they weren't so bothered about him shaving his head regularly.

"Can I help?" he stuttered, seemingly unused to speaking much anymore. He approached the staircase, placing one bony hand on the balustrade.

"I'm not sure. You're 1?" He nodded, taking a step down, using the bannister to support his weight as he lowered himself down on his single leg. He looked nervous as he stood there, thumb in his pocket.

"I am. It's been quite some time since anybody ventured up here to talk to me. I have my own room, take my meals separately … I keep myself to myself." He scratched his head. I couldn't blame the guy – what he'd been through, it's no wonder he'd completely withdrawn.

"What is it you do in here?" I asked, genuinely curious.

"Well, I read, obviously. I can't be much help, but I have been tasked with finding out anything I can about creatures similar to the Saurians, anything to do with infectious diseases and the odd other little project. The scientists take my research from time to time." He seemed proud of this fact; I suppose he needed to feel like he still had some purpose.

"To be honest, I think I've largely been forgotten about, and it's probably safer if that's the way things stay. I wouldn't want the powers-that-be to start asking questions about just how useful I am."

He probably had a point – in Myla's eyes, he'd be a dead weight, a drain on resources. I hoped for his sake he kept his head down and avoided her scrutiny. It seemed a safe bet that she'd simply forgotten he even existed; it would explain why he was still alive.

"I don't want to take up too much of your time," I started, as he shook his head to say no problem, and waved me into a seat. He clumsily stepped down the remaining stairs to take a chair opposite.

"A friend of mine suggested I come and talk to you. It's a bit of a delicate matter –"

He held his hand up. "You really do not have to be concerned about my telling anyone your business," he said gently.

"I don't want to upset you, or bring up something you're not comfortable with, but –"

"But it's important," he finished for me. "I'm not surprised. I always half expected someone to seek me out. What do you need to know?"

"Have you ever heard of a place, a city, where they have a different way of life? And perhaps even a vaccine?" I held my breath, anxious to hear his response. He looked me square in the eyes for several minutes.

"Once," he said when he finally spoke. "On my last trip as a runner."

Subconsciously, his hand went to his chest where I glimpsed, just below his t-shirt, a vivid red scar.

"Even then, we went out in pairs, so it was me and a guy we called Starbucks, the name of an old coffee shop, because he always seemed wired. A couple of hours outside the wall, we came across a village with a small group of survivors barricaded in an old public house. They'd been told about a city in the south – Anex? Amex?"

"Amex, I think."

He nodded. "They made it sound like a land of dreams. We were shocked when we saw them, as they were Xs and Ys living together. Urged us to come with them, or at least follow on. They even drew us a map to direct us, following the safest known route. They weren't sure of the distance, but it was clearly going to be a long trip."

"Did you go with them?"

"That was the plan. It seemed like a no-brainer, a chance we couldn't turn down. I mean, would you?"

I thought back to my pre-Cara life. An opportunity to escape the division and control of Galex? He was right, it took very little thinking about. I shook my head.

"I'd have jumped at it. But you're back here. What happened – couldn't you find Amex?"

"We didn't even get the chance to try. We agreed to accompany them, but we were wary too: they were, after all, strangers in a dangerous landscape. So while they stayed the night in the public house, we took the barn. It was fairly ramshackle, but it was dry at least and with our heads filled with the fantasy of a new life, we didn't expect to get a lot of sleep anyway."

"We must have dozed off though, because it was shrieks and screams of pain that woke us."

He covered his eyes with his hand. "We'd never actually come face to face with a Saurian, despite being sent out on multiple missions. We wavered between hiding, quaking in fear, and fleeing for our lives. From the sounds we heard, the idea of mounting an attack seemed impossible. Cowardly, I know," he added, fixing me with another direct stare, challenging me to agree. I could see flecks of gold in his irises.

I shook myself from the vision he had conjured. "Not at all. I saw them kill my friend Blue. Watched them rip him apart. I stayed hidden – knew it would be suicide to try and help. He was dead already." I knew I was speaking the truth, yet my words still rang hollow; the scene of his death replayed in my head for the hundredth time. Could I have saved him?

Brown 1 clearly recognised my guilt as the same he shared. A sense of comradeship warmed his eyes.

"So you understand. Anyway, we chose to flee. We crept out of the barn and ran as fast as we could back towards the city. I only glimpsed what was going on in the public house, but it looked like there were at least four Saurians, and they made light work of the group."

He paused again, clearly reluctant to go on with his story.

"Of course, we didn't make it back in one piece," he continued, gesturing to his missing leg.

"One of them must have followed us. It pounced about 400 metres from the walls. It got Starbucks first, grappled him to the ground with no more effort than a cat playing with a toy."

His eyes were glassy suddenly, as he relived the horror. His hand dragged itself down to his neck and the gold in his eyes shone out even more.

"I stood helpless for a few seconds, before I did the only thing I could – not to save him, I knew it was too late for that, but to give myself a chance to get away. I took my hunting knife and jammed it through the Saurian's eyes, trying to pierce both."

The hunting knife he was talking about was pretty unimpressive in size, but sharp enough to cut through bone. I looked at him admiringly – this had been a clever plan, and had obviously saved his life.

"As you can see, it worked, because I'm alive. But it wasn't a perfect escape. The beast was blinded, but enraged. It lashed out, and I wasn't quite quick enough to get out of range. It grabbed me by the calf and bit down. Hard."

I shuddered. The brute strength behind this must have been incredible.

"It was agony, of course," Brown 1 continued, noting my horrified expression. "I nearly gave up there and then. But I managed to drag myself out of reach when it loosened its jaws, and I kept moving until I could see the walls."

"It didn't follow?"

He shrugged, lost in the memory. "It tried briefly to find me, but not for long. It had a meal that wasn't moving, so it settled for that. I was lucky," he laughed mirthlessly.

I didn't join in. The parallels with my own experience were clear. I realised how lucky I'd been to get up close to the Saurians and come away unscathed. Physically, at least.

"When I got back," he carried on, "the obvious thing to

do was amputate my leg. It was pretty mangled anyway, and there was a fear that I'd be infected and could mutate." He stared at the space where his leg used to be. "I was closely monitored, left to heal. When it became clear I wasn't going to turn lizardy, the scientists let me come up here. I imagine they were curious to see if there were any long-term side effects of such an attack. I'm an interesting case study, I suppose."

He shrugged. "After that, I never left the city again." He gave me another unflinching stare. "Couldn't face it."

I sat back and sighed heavily. "Can't say I'm surprised," I answered, shaking my head to try and dislodge the gruesome images he'd conjured in my mind.

We sat in silence for a while, before my mind settled on an earlier detail from his story. "The map they drew for you – what happened to that?" I inquired, jolted back to my own reality by the possibility of an escape route.

"Burnt it," he answered simply. "Couldn't risk it falling into the wrong hands."

My heart fell.

"Of course, I memorised it first," he said, smiling slyly. "Would you like me to draw you a copy?"

I left the library soon after, clutching a small piece of paper with a crude map crayoned on it. It seemed like a long shot, if I'm honest, but at least it was something. I had to hope that there was a better world out there – for me, for Cara, and now for our baby. If there was a chance we could live together as a family, I would have to take it.

CARA

EIGHT

My heart nearly broke when I saw Brown arrive for the debriefing. Eyes reddened, limping, he looked exhausted. All I wanted to do was put my arms around him.

Myla was her usual self around them. She goaded the runners, hoping for a reaction, an excuse. Luckily, Brown knew enough not to let her get to him, though I could tell she'd ruffled his feathers. I sensed he was angry with me, too – I suppose I could understand that. He'd just seen his best friend viciously murdered, and none of us acted like anything much had even happened. If I were in his shoes, I'd be raging. I resolved to go and see him that night, just quickly, to tell him how sorry I was for his loss.

Once the runners had gone, I stood up to leave, expecting the meeting to be over. Myla seemed unconcerned by the reports, so I guessed that was it.

Turns out not. She dismissed the recruits and beckoned over two of our scientists, Orla and Mags. They perched nervously, white coats setting them apart from the rest of us. I was surprised to see them: Myla was normally pretty dismissive of their work, preferring to focus on brute force instead.

"D'you hear all that?" she barked at them.

Mags nodded sagely. "It's as we suspected. The creatures are evolving."

I turned to Myla. "What? You knew about this? You just told those two Ys it was nothing much!"

She shot me a raised eyebrow. "Well, obviously I'm not going to share my thoughts and fears with the help!" She spluttered indignantly. In a calmer tone, she added, "We had suspicions. Recent reports have suggested the Saurians were developing, but it wasn't clear how quickly. Today's report is concerning – it seems they're advancing faster than expected."

"Why didn't you tell me this before?" I asked, slightly hurt at being left out of the loop.

"It was info strictly on a need-to-know basis, Little Sis," Myla shrugged, loving the fact that she knew more than me. "I've left you in charge of the attack plans. How are they coming along, by the way?"

"Fine," I answered quickly, feeling slightly guilty that the plans had been put on the back burner whilst I'd been coming to terms with being pregnant. "Still just preparing the recruits for the kind of warfare they'll be up against."

"It might turn out that you've got less to do than we previously thought," Myla spoke quietly, checking the room was unoccupied apart from our small group before she continued.

"What progress have you made?" she addressed Mags.

"Quite a lot," she responded with a hint of pride in her

voice, tortoiseshell glasses frames resting on the tip of her nose. "We've tested three subjects now, and the results are the same each time. The formula created acts as a vaccine."

"What now?" I shouted, my heart in my mouth. Were they discussing what I thought they were discussing? "A vaccine? For the Epidemic?"

Mags looked at Myla, who nodded. "In effect, yes. We synthesised it from test subjects and have been refining it. Shylah had the basics of it – we've just taken her work a step further."

The use of the pronoun 'we' wasn't lost on me – trust Myla to take credit for the scientists' discovery as if it were her own. It clearly wasn't lost on Orla either, whose pursed lips quietly betrayed her annoyance at the lack of credit.

"Do you understand what this means?" I said, still reeling from this breakthrough.

"We do," said Myla. "The end to the Saurian threat."

"But not just that," I went on, hope filling me. "This could mean the Ys can live among us again. If the Epidemic can't mutate them –"

"Hang on a minute," Orla interrupted. "It's not that simple."

"It's not?" I asked in disbelief.

"Unfortunately not," continued Mags, pushing her spectacles further up her nose. "There's a problem. We've tried and tried to solve it, but so far … no luck."

"What's the problem? Don't tell me it's something stupid, like a worry that another virus will come along and do the same thing?!"

"No," said Myla briskly. "The vaccine. It kills the Ys. It

111

stops them mutating, but kills them anyway."

Mags picked up from Myla's blunt words. "Not straight away," she added gently. "They seem fine, feel strong even. We really thought we'd cracked it. But then, after a few days, they drop dead. It seems that this vaccine poisons their blood as a side effect to destroying the DNA mutation."

Disappointment plummeted through me. The thought of a vaccine had briefly given me a future, one with Brown – that had just been cruelly snatched away.

"You're sure?" I asked, clinging on to a remnant of hope. Surely this meant they were close to a real solution?

"We are," answered Orla, her curly blonde hair bouncing as she nodded solemnly. "Like we said, three subjects have now died. I mean, we can keep testing but … I'm quite sure it'd be pointless."

"It's getting harder to keep all this quiet too," said Myla. "I can't risk the rest of the Ys finding out about this."

"But why the secrecy?" I questioned. "Surely we're trying to help them? We've just not got it quite right yet. Giving them some hope might be a good thing!" I would love to be able to give this to Brown – a ray of light in what must be a dark time for him.

"Well that's just it," laughed Myla. "Helping them was never my intention, Sis. I couldn't give two hoots about them – whether they live, die, or grow five heads each. I'd be tempted to rid us of the lot of them, if it weren't for the small matter of keeping the human race alive."

I turned to Mags, hoping for a clearer answer.

"We were trying to find a way to regulate the mutations. We figured that if we could create Saurians, we could use them – our own personal army. That's why we're interested in the evolution of the beasts: we wanted to know if we could control them."

I couldn't believe what I was hearing. I stared at my sister, as if seeing her clearly for the first time. "Even for you, Myla, this is too far. You'd risk the lives of everyone here? And for what?"

"Wouldn't it be better to send out a Saurian army than our own recruits?" she justified, eyes flashing when she saw the expression on my face. "Don't give me that look, Sis! You know I'd protect this community no matter what, but we have to be ready. If the Saurians evolve, we need a powerful enough weapon to attack them, which won't mean the deaths of Xs!" She looked genuinely hurt. "If I can harness a new weapon, I will. Regardless of any collateral damage. Who's looking out for us, if not me?"

It was clear that the 'us' she spoke about were Xs – to Myla, Ys were not even a factor worth considering, merely 'collateral damage'. Her total lack of emotion towards the Ys left me with an emptiness inside: I realised I had no choice but to get Brown away from my sister for good.

"But was this not incredibly risky?" I continued, still flabbergasted. "If you create Saurians, they could run wild, kill us all. You could have created an even stronger creature, that for all you knew, was beyond your control."

"Don't underestimate me, Cara," Myla responded darkly, her eyes still on mine.

"We took precautions," Orla defended, clearly put out that I was questioning her abilities as a scientist. "We were careful. However, as it turns out, we managed to remove whatever genetic trait turns them into Saurians. It's just a shame they apparently can't live without it."

I thought about this. "So, the experiment failed? So, that's it?" I guessed I should feel relief. Brown hadn't been tested on, and the tests were clearly useless, so, surely he should be safe until I could get him out of the city?

"Not entirely," Myla said. My heart sank, as I felt a sense of dread about what was coming next. "We will keep trying. But the other tests? How did they go?"

"Much better," said Mags, clearly glad to be the bearer of more positive news. "They went exactly as we predicted."

"Excellent. Does this mean we can continue with the mission as planned?"

Both scientists nodded.

"Is someone going to fill me in?" I demanded, annoyed at being a step behind again.

"We ran some other tests," Mags began to elaborate, her hand gestures revealing her excitement at their success. "Our aim was always to get rid of the Saurian threat. Therefore, when controlling mutations proved beyond us for the time being, we wondered if there was another way."

"And?"

"We found one."

*

Then

When I did that first pregnancy test, I felt numb. It was sort of like an out-of-body experience – this couldn't be happening to me; this wasn't the plan! I'd already been so reckless – starting a relationship with Brown, risking everything for him. I genuinely didn't know what Myla would do if she found out – it was a severe breach of the rules to have any form of unauthorised contact with a Y. I dreaded to think how she'd punish Brown.

I basically ignored it for about a month. Kind of like, if I didn't think about it, it wasn't happening. Fairly childish, I know. But what could I do? I considered getting rid of it – but how? Who could I get to help me? What if it went wrong?

I remember feeling so alone. I desperately wanted to tell Brown: after all, this was his baby too – but I couldn't get my own head around it yet. And what if we disagreed about what to do? I couldn't think straight myself: it seemed unfair to burden him with such a massive bombshell before I'd had chance to come to terms with it. I owed him that, at least.

It was around this time that I had to make my annual visit to the State Institute for Children. I do realise how forbidding this place sounds – like an old-fashioned orphanage where kids are neglected or chained to cots. Thankfully, it's a lot better than that – it's more like what I imagine nurseries used to be like. As family units no longer existed, the institute was where any baby Xs were taken soon after birth. They grew up here together, learning necessary skills, developing their personalities. Their mothers could visit as often as they liked – these children were loved. The whole community felt a responsibility in bringing them up – helping them to develop, build relationships and learn how to adapt to Galex society.

Every year, part of my job was to head down and take a look at the different age groups, see who was already looking likely to be future recruits. Some of the older ones would be on the cusp of puberty, and nearly ready to begin training. I enjoyed the visits: the cheery walls covered in posters and pictures were bright and added life that was often lacking in a soldier's dorm. Aged around four and five, the younger girls were still years away from training, but the nurses who ran the Institute were well practised in spotting talent early on.

"Welcome back, Protector," Nurse Thelma greeted me, with a warm handshake. Thelma had been running the place from the beginning – now in her fifties, she was one of the older members of the community.

"Please, call me Cara," I said again. We went through this ritual every year. I knew she never would address me by my first name, but I couldn't help but try. I hated the hierarchy that seemed to define Galex nowadays.

"I think you'll be impressed with this year's students," she continued as if I hadn't spoken, brushing a few wisps of greying hair out of her face. The rest of it had been pulled back into her usual severe bun. "Quite a number of them seem to have an aptitude for fighting." I had to listen extra carefully – originally from Scotland, Thelma still had quite a strong accent.

"Is that so?"

"It certainly is. Some of them are very spirited indeed." Thelma's downturned mouth told me she disapproved of this. I imagined it could be fairly tricky to control a riotous bunch of kids all day every day. From my perspective, though, it was great – I needed courage, fire and energy to shape promising recruits. The routine and hardships of training soon knocked even the liveliest into shape.

"So, you'll have your hands full then," I stated rather than asked.

"Aye, indeed," she said drily, with a wry smile.

She led me into the playroom, where a group of about seven children were entertaining themselves. It was amazing how you could see who would have what skills, even at this age. One was climbing across furniture; a couple of others were building elaborate towers. One sat reading in the corner, whilst the rest seemed engaged in a complicated game of warfare.

I stood watching, taking it all in.

"Children!" Thelma shouted, clapping her hands. After a small burst of protest, they all downed tools and headed over.

"I'd like you to meet our City Protector," Thelma announced proudly. "She's here to take a look at you and see if any of you could one day become one of the brave ones who look after us all and stop anything bad happening inside the city walls." The children made noises of admiration, and crowded round to ask questions.

"Do you fight the lizard men?"

"How many have you killed?"

"What weapons do you have?"

"How do I get to be a fighter?"

Laughing, I answered them all as best I could – it was far too early to say which ones would be selected at the age of ten, but it was great to see this initial enthusiasm, and to start letting the nurses prepare some more fully.

My visit lasted a couple of hours. On my way out, I paused by the child who had stayed reading all throughout my time there.

"You okay?" I asked her. She looked up at me with liquid brown eyes, and shrugged.

"I just don't like fighting," she answered quietly.

Kneeling down, I replied, "That's okay. Not everybody is good at the same things. What do you like?"

"I like learning and reading." She thought hard. "I also like cheese."

I laughed.

"Me too! Well, it sounds like there will be plenty of other things you can do when you're older – maybe help the scientists, or write the Galex journal which tells all about our world for future generations to read."

"Really?" she answered, so hopeful as she looked up at me. "I don't have to fight?"

"Of course not. We all do what we're good at."

On my way out, for the first time, I realised I didn't want to fight anymore either. It was time to do something different.

Speaking with the girls, seeing their hopes and dreams, also helped make my decision for me. I was going to keep this baby. I wanted to be the one who made them feel better, and who helped their dreams come true.

Even if it meant I had to leave Galex, I couldn't give this baby up.

*

Now

It wasn't until I got back to my room later that night, that I could let out all the emotions I'd been holding in since the meeting with the scientists. I sank to the floor and wept. Never had I felt so helpless. Myla's plan was efficient. It made sense. Or, at least, it did if you didn't mind sacrificing the lives of Ys for the good of the Xs.

The scientists' solution had been explained without emotion.

"We knew we had a vaccine which had a genetic effect. It stopped mutations. Unfortunately, it also killed the host. But then we starting to ask, what effect would it have on an already transformed Saurian?"

"It was a really interesting question," enthused Orla. "And we were delighted when we found a way to test it."

"How did you get away with secretly infecting the Saurians with a vaccine? Surely that was a dangerous, reckless mission you sent some poor Ys on!" I asked indignantly.

"Why must you always stick up for them?" sighed Myla, shaking her head at me in disbelief. "They killed our mother!" she spat.

"Not exactly," I retorted. "To be honest, they're as much victims in this as we are. It's not their fault they're more susceptible to this virus than we are."

"Careful, Sis," she warned. "Don't let your bleeding heart show too much. Somebody might rip it out."

I turned my attention back to the scientists, determined not to let Myla rile me, or to give too much of myself away. "So, how did you manage to test the vaccine on a Saurian?"

"It was quite clever, actually," boasted Mags, obviously the author of the idea. "We had three dead Ys, seemingly useless. But then we thought: what would a Saurian do, if it came across their bodies? The answer?"

"Eat them," I mumbled, suddenly realising what they'd done.

"Precisely! Gold star to you!" Mags obviously thought she was being funny, but I just scowled at her, sickened by the way she was talking about three dead human beings as if they were no more than an ingredient in a science experiment. "We sent a small team of trusted recruits out, hand-picked by your sister. They were instructed to take the bodies and dump them just near to a small nest discovered on the west side of the city. We made up a story about the bodies being infected with the virus and needing to get them far away from Galex. And then we waited."

The thought of it was pretty horrible. Three carcasses left out for the creatures to feed on. The mental image was disturbing.

"So ... what happened?" Despite my disgust, I was curious.

"We sent two runners the following week to scout out the nest. Made an excuse about Saurians attacking each other, and wanting to see if they'd been at war. When they returned, they said the whole nest had been wiped out. They counted eight rotting bodies, dissolving in pools of black blood."

"What this means," Myla elaborated for me, "is that the greedy bastards ate the bodies and poisoned themselves. And, voila, we have a way to kill our enemies."

"Meaning the Saurians?" I questioned, suddenly afraid.

"I see it as two birds, one stone," she said, shamelessly looking me in the eyes, her dark irises free from emotion. "Dead Saurians, dead Ys. It's a win, win."

"Are you telling me your plan is to murder the Ys, and leave their bodies for the Saurians to feast on?" This was a shocking plan, even by Myla's standards.

"Not quite. We infect the Ys, send them out to help in the battle against the Saurians. We then wait for them to die and feed them to the Saurians, or speed up the process by letting the beasts kill and eat them. Either way, the Saurians end up poisoned, and there's a few less Ys cluttering up the city. Not a bad plan, hey?"

"Myla, we can't do this!"

"What choice do we have, Sis? Ultimately, if the Saurians attack in their new organised form, we will be in serious trouble. We must strike first and if it comes down to us or the Ys dying, I'd rather it was them."

*

Once Myla had revealed the true extent of the upcoming mission, I had to get out of there. My heart was pounding, I felt sick and my legs were wobbly. The way she spoke was truly terrifying – she thought no more of sending the Ys to their deaths than she would of swatting an annoying fly. I couldn't stop seeing that look in her eyes: a coldness that betrayed her complete lack of emotion. This was going to happen – unless I did something to stop it.

But what could I do? The mission had been my idea.

Brown would blame me – if he survived. As it stood, he had already unwittingly volunteered to be Saurian bait.

I realised that I could not let that happen. No matter what. Somehow, I was going to have to stop the Ys being injected, yet still make sure that the Saurian threat was defeated.

And it was becoming increasingly clear that I could no longer stay in Galex, especially while my sister was in charge.

MYLA

NINE

Cara has a tell. When she's lying, her left ey
doesn't lie to me often, but this tell means
does, I always know. She's lying to me now.

I've suspected something's been going
She's been … weird. Getting more liberal arc
throwing herself into training to the same e>
she's got me fooled, but I miss nothing.

I've been watching her closely. I've kn
about her secret lover, having found myse'
spy once Ilana proved to be a disappointmer
matter of time before I deal with him in the
He will be made an example of. There is nc
am to safeguard the fate of this community

*

Twelve seconds. That's how long it took
change. To mutate. We stood in the livi:

ave. Trying to get out, get anywhere, before it was too late.
had been me who'd begged mum to let him come with
. He'd been so grateful, had hugged me so tight. I could
ill see Mum's eyes though. The doubt she felt. But who can
ny the innocent wish of a child, whose love for her daddy
as pure as snow?

It was Cara he went for. She was so little, just sitting in
e corner, wailing about leaving her favourite toys behind.
um almost didn't notice until it was too late, as her back
s turned to him while she comforted Cara.

I saw every second of it though, and my brain counted
m down, like a really messed up New Year's Eve
untdown. Only to a much worse world.

12. Dad started scratching. 11. He shook loose his
lar. 10. Began pulling his clothing, desperate to escape it.
. Skin writhing, like an alien waiting to burst out from
ide. 7, 6. Eyes bloodshot. Face gone. 5, 4. Dad gone. A
nster in his place, ready to pounce. It was only now that
reamed.

3. Mum looked up. Concern for Cara transformed to
olute terror.

2. Cara went quiet, staring up at this creature, as it lunged
ards her.

1. I threw myself in front of her, screeching at what had
e been my Dad, to stop, go away!

It was only luck that the army officers in the street heard
a's wailing. Only by chance they'd come to the window
e what the commotion was. Pure good fortune that one
his gun trained on the beast just as it jumped.

And dumb luck he got it straight in the skull.

A knock at the office door disturbed me.

"Come in!"

It was my spy.

"Tyra, I was just thinking about you." The girl blushed. She looked immensely guilty, as she always did when she came to me with information. I'd worked hard to convince her she was doing this for Cara's own good, otherwise I knew she'd never betray her like this. I'd given the whole, 'Ys are so manipulative' speech. 'You wouldn't want to see Cara in trouble, would you?' 'It'll never last. He'll only hurt her – best to nip it in the bud before that can happen.'

"What have you for me?" I asked, keen to keep the meeting short. I hadn't the time to make her feel better about herself today, and her usefulness was nearing an end, what with the upcoming mission.

"She went to him again, two nights ago," she quietly told me. "I was on duty at the door, so I followed her. They were in the usual place – bottom of the kitchen garden."

"And?" I demanded, irritated at this seemingly uninteresting piece of news.

"Something was different. More intense," she added quickly, perhaps seeing my impatience.

"How so?"

"Just the way he looked at her and held her. They looked really happy, but also really scared. It seemed like they were planning something."

I sat up. This was more interesting. "Thank you," I told her. "Anything else?"

"Just that I heard her tell him not to volunteer for the upcoming mission. I think she wants to protect him," she added.

"Don't worry, I think I've solved that problem," I said confidently. With the death of his friend and my humiliation of him, I knew this Brown would be hell bent on volunteering, no matter what the risk.

"Now I just need you to be particularly vigilant," I finished. "I must know of any further meetings and ideally, I need you to eavesdrop on their conversation."

Tyra looked miserable and uncomfortable. "It's not always possible," she protested. "I have tried –"

"Well try harder," I retorted icily. Eyes on her feet, her face blanched.

I knew my reputation among the recruits. It had been well earned. I used it now to intimidate her. "This is vital. It might save Cara's life."

With this, I'd got her. "I'll try my best," she said, chin set in determination.

I had to admire her loyalty, I thought as she let herself out, doing all this to protect her mentor. I'd learnt long ago that you had to make difficult choices and do unsavoury things in this world. It was the only way to keep control. To keep us safe.

*

Since that moment when fate spared us from my father, I knew I had to protect Cara. She was my responsibility, even when Mum was alive. I had made a mistake in trusting Dad, but I wouldn't make that mistake again. I couldn't. Cara had been spared and so had I. The problem was that she didn't remember. Hadn't experienced that feeling when the person you love the most turns on you. When they transform into a monster that would destroy you in a heartbeat. I had to protect her from herself, from her naivety. You can't love a Y, not fully, because you don't know what they could become.

The next few weeks will be critical, though. Now Cara knows the planned fate for the Ys sent on the mission, including her beloved Brown, it will allow me to test her – just how far is she willing to go to protect him? I can't let her make the same mistake I did when I was a child. For her own sake, but also for the sake of Galex.

I sensed there was more to this than I yet realised and resolved to keep even closer tabs on them both. It was imperative that he went on that mission, and that he died as planned.

BROWN

TEN

Red and Orange were as depressed as I was the following morning.

"I still can't believe he's gone!" exclaimed Orange, using his spoon to play with his sloppy porridge, without eating any of it. "He was always so full of life."

"I know, man," nodded Red. "He wolfed down anything we brought him, whilst complaining about it obviously," he chuckled sadly.

"It was so horrible," I intoned. "I wouldn't have wished that fate on anyone."

"Not anyone?" asked Orange, a quick glance around to make sure we weren't overheard. "Not even the Boss?" he whispered.

I looked at him sharply. Even thinking that kind of thing was risky. Saying it out loud was seriously dangerous.

"Careful!" Red hissed. Then, barely above a whisper, he leaned into me. "A small group of us are meeting tonight, just after lights out. If you want things to change, be there."

*

It was dangerous. Any form of meeting or gathering was strictly forbidden and harshly punished. I'm talking floggings, or worse. Under no circumstances did they want us Ys getting together and talking, planning. Any hint of dissent was quickly smashed with an iron fist.

Regardless, I spent the day thinking about whether or not to join tonight's meeting. I was lucky to have a day of recuperation after yesterday's horrors, so I had plenty of time with my thoughts. I missed Blue as a friend, and a confidante. I'd so wanted to tell him about Cara and the baby, but now I'd never get the chance.

I was conflicted about Cara, too. I knew she wanted to see me, and part of me really wanted to see her. I'm pretty sure I'd heard her signalling last night, with a pitter patter of stones against the window. My heart ached though, especially when I looked at the empty bed to my left. For the first time ever, I ignored her. I couldn't face talking about what had happened, or even thinking about a future in this world.

The way things were, in this place – they couldn't continue like this. We couldn't be together in a world where my friends were lizard food, and no one cared. Worse, the leader of Galex actively encouraged it. And she was Cara's sister.

I was sick of being humiliated and treated as worthless. Of being made to feel that, as a Y, my life didn't matter. I was fed up with being treated as the enemy.

Things had to change.

But at the same time, I knew I couldn't abandon her now. With a baby. My baby. More than that, I didn't *want* to abandon them. I needed to be there for them, but I also needed to be able to help them. If that meant risking my life on a mission, then so be it. At least if I were dead, Cara could make up some story about where the baby had come from.

Plus, I loved Cara. I really did. Despite our differences, despite the fact we couldn't openly be together, it felt like we were meant to be. When I was with her, it felt … right. I was angry at the system, yes, and sometimes that anger transferred onto her – but I knew it wasn't her fault, not really. I got the fact that even if she stood up to her sister, it wouldn't make things any better, and it could make them worse.

Part of me still wished she would, though. I couldn't shake the feeling that at some point, she was going to be forced to make a choice.

And then recently, the rumours about Amex, the map from Brown 1 – they had given me hope. If we could get away, if we survived … there was a chance we could build a better life together.

It had occurred to me that if we were going to make things happen, it had to be now. What if the baby was a boy? I didn't think I could bear to see my child grow up under this regime, being treated like he was nothing.

It was this last thought which made my mind up – I would go to the meeting and see what they had to say.

*

Before

I was 10 when the city turned against us. I remember the fear we all felt when we found out two Ys had turned. Hysteria grew and infected everyone. We were terrified – were we next? The Xs were terrified – would more change? When we were herded together and left in the old gym, it seemed fairly sensible. Keep us together, under lock and key, until they could find out what was going on.

Except that they didn't really ever find out. The safety precautions became more like punishments for the deaths of the Founders. To Gloria, we were all to blame.

Even when we were released, things weren't much better. The first thing to go was our names.

"It doesn't matter who you were," Gloria announced, gun in hand. "You're now just a commodity and will be categorised as such. Any trust you had is gone. Any freedom you had is gone. Any identity you had is gone. From now on, you will have a job and that will define you."

"And think yourselves lucky things aren't worse for you," added Myla, her eyes harder than ever. "This is mercy. If I were in charge, you'd all be gone for good this time."

The look in her eyes left no doubt that she meant it. Gloria was angry, that much was clear: but Myla spoke from something beyond emotion. She had crossed a line and now, to her, Ys weren't people. Weren't human. We were the enemy.

*

After

We gathered in the toilets after lights out. Not the most glamorous of locations, but needs must. It was the only place the Xs were pretty much guaranteed not to go.

Red had shuffled past my bunk, then I followed after a couple of minutes. By the time I got there, there were four others crammed in by the sinks – Red, Orange, and Browns 6 and 8. I nodded to them.

"Glad to see you," greeted 6, with a slap on my back. I wasn't surprised to see him here – after what we'd witnessed, anyone would be wanting to find a way out.

Stood opposite the sinks in front of the stalls, was Brown 12, seemingly in charge. Stooping and slim, with earnest eyes and a downturned mouth, he had that serious edge that made people sit up and listen. It hadn't stopped us nicknaming him Eeyore after some sad-looking donkey, though.

"Thanks for coming," he said quietly, "I appreciate the risks, so I'll keep this as short as possible."

"There's a growing number of Ys who feel that the time has come to start fighting back. Things have been getting worse and worse for us, and we've decided enough is enough." Eeyore clenched his fists, squaring his jaw. I remembered he'd been on the receiving end of one of Myla's tempers when he'd come back with bad news from a mission.

"It's time to take action." The others nodded, 6 looking as determined as Eeyore did.

"You're right, man," he said, enthused. "If we don't,

we're finished." He turned to me. "Did you see the look in the Boss' eyes yesterday? She hates us. Like, really hates us. She won't stop at nothing."

"It's true," I agreed, facing the others. "We told her we'd seen the deaths of our friends and she couldn't give a toss. Just tried to wind us up so we'd react, and give her an excuse to attack us too." My blood boiled just thinking about it.

"She's the reason we need to act now. Myla hates Ys. To her, we are and always will be a threat. I honestly don't think she'll stop until she's destroyed us all." We lapsed into silence, considering the gravity of Eeyore's statement.

"So, a plan is coming together. There's a group of us – I'm the representative sent to recruit you guys; others are being recruited by different members. The idea is to keep this as secret as possible, so if anyone is caught or suspected, they can't give everyone away."

"Makes sense," added Red.

"I need to know now if you're in," Eeyore continued. "It's fine if you don't want any part of it, just swear a vow of silence and you can carry on with your miserable existence. If you say you're in though, there's no going back. You will be given a role that you'll need to complete, to save letting down the rest of us and possibly getting fellow Ys killed."

"Obviously, we're in," whispered Orange. "Who in our situation wouldn't be?"

"You haven't heard the plan yet," clarified Eeyore. "Things might change when you do."

An air of mystery hung about him. Irritated by this showmanship, I said, "Come on then, out with it. We can't stand about in here forever."

Eeyore turned his gaze on me, his downcast eyes seemingly disappointed with my impatience.

"The plan is to get rid of Myla. It's the only way to start a chain reaction of change. She's too dangerous and too blinkered to keep power. If we are ever to be safe, she has to die. And," here he paused, clearly not willing to let go of the tension just yet, "we have to be prepared to kill more Xs too."

*

Before

The last days with my mum seemed like a distant memory once our world changed after the deaths of the Founders. Her weakness at the end, my own helplessness. I just sat for hours by her side, watching her chest rise and fall slowly. Her breaths seemed to grow shallower every hour.

Her last morning: we both knew the end was close. Her skin tone had greyed, and her lips were completely bloodless. She grasped my hand weakly, her squeeze of my fingers feeling more like the brush of a feather.

"Keep living, son," she whispered, her voice fading along with the rest of her.

"Don't live in fear because of what you are, and never give up." Her eyes shone with momentary ferocity as she gripped my hand with all her remaining strength.

"Remember that the only things that really matter in this life are the ones you love. Protect them with everything you've got." She sank back into her pillows, relieved to have said her piece.

"Don't worry, Mum, I'll remember," I answered, putting her hand to my lips for a final kiss.

She closed her eyes and sighed for the last time.

*

After

Back in my bunk, I thought back over Eeyore's words. Murdering Myla – it was definitely a bold plan, and possibly a really stupid one. I hoped they weren't underestimating her cunning.

Eeyore hadn't had much time to elaborate on any details, as he was worried we'd be noticed as missing if we congregated for too long. He simply outlined the main idea to attack Myla when most of the recruits were out on the upcoming mission. The Ys would overthrow society immediately, imprison any resistant Xs and then wait for the returning recruits. They suspected they wouldn't all come back and those that did would be tired and weak after battling the Saurians.

"If we obtain control of the main building and the weaponry, we should be able to take them," Eeyore said confidently.

"And if not?" I asked, feeling uncomfortable at the thought of Cara returning home to a violent coup.

He shrugged casually. "We take a few more lives to prove we mean business."

"Doesn't this just make us as bad as her?" I questioned, feeling panic rising at this further divisionary idea.

"It's the only language they'll understand," emphasised Eeyore. "Plus, I'd love to get revenge on some of them. They've enjoyed lording it over us – now it's our turn."

I shook my head, feeling more than ever like I had no understanding of most people.

"So, who's in?"

"I am," Red answered straight away. I look at him, surprised. "What? It's them or us. Dog eat dog," he expanded.

"Me too," said Orange quickly.

"And you two?" Eeyore turned to us remaining runners.

"We'll likely be out on the mission," 6 said, "but if I can help from there, I will."

"We might need you to keep the recruits out there for as long as possible, give us time to establish control."

Finally, Eeyore turned to me. "And you?"

I paused. Everything in me was screaming not to have any part in this. Replacing one dictatorship with another was not something I wanted to be a part of. However, if I could find a way to protect Cara, it would be worth being in the know.

"I'm in," I replied eventually. "And I might have an idea about what role I could play."

*

As the others went back to bed after the meeting, Eeyore held me back.

"You sure you're up for this?" He looked concerned, clearly worried I was going to back out at the last minute.

I steeled myself. "Things need to change," I repeated his words stubbornly.

He nodded slowly, apparently mollified. "What's your idea?"

I took a deep breath, sucking in my courage. I had to play this right. "I've been on a few missions with Cara, the Protector. I reckon I could overpower her outside the walls, away from the other recruits. Bring her back separately. She's the most likely X to stick up for her sister, so if I get her out of the way, she won't pose a threat."

He stared at me again. I kept my expression neutral. "Nice idea," he acquiesced eventually. "Bring her here so we can make an example of her, too."

"Not necessarily," I added quickly. "She's not as bad as her sister, she might fall in line."

Eeyore laughed humourlessly. "Doubtful. Whatever though, the others look up to her. They'd follow her lead if she gave us her support. I guess we just don't give her much of an option. She either supports us, or, she ends up like her sister." And with that, he patted me on the back and left.

I stood there like an idiot, hoping against hope that I hadn't just thrown Cara to the wolves.

*

I dreamt wildly that night. I was being chased by Myla, who morphed into Cara, who turned into a Saurian. Just as I was about to be eaten, I turned into Blue and punched, waking up in a fight with my blankets.

Lying back, the events of last night came back to me. The plot. Myla. Don't get me wrong, I certainly had no loyalty or love for our leader. In fact, the opposite was true. She was a cruel and vicious bully, with a serious chip on her shoulder where Ys were concerned. I'd be delighted to find out she'd been abducted by aliens in the night, leaving Galex Myla-free. However, this didn't mean that I agreed with murdering her. I couldn't help but think that even if this plan succeeded, things wouldn't actually be that different. There would still be those in control and those who were controlled. The fear of mutating would still be there. My relationship with Cara would still be forbidden. I also couldn't bear the thought of her being caught up in it and given the same fate as her sister.

I also couldn't live with the thought of being part of a plot to kill Cara's sister, no matter what I thought of her. It simply wasn't fair – I couldn't do that to Cara. My only hope was to stay informed about the plan and use it to keep Cara safe.

In the cold light of day, it was clear what I had to do. I'd agreed to kidnap Cara on the mission. I could still be seen to do that. However, I had no intention of bringing her back to face a braying mob, after revenge for years of mistreatment. I would be seen to kidnap her, sure – but in fact, it would be a rescue. Once away, we'd be free to head for Amex and take our chances there.

Hope lit inside me: I could see it working! Cara would go along with it now, because of the baby. If she wanted to keep it, and if she wanted me in her life, we would have no choice but to leave Galex. I doubted she'd need much convincing.

The only sticking point was Myla. There was still a plan in place to murder her, and despite their differences of opinion, I knew Cara couldn't walk away knowing that was going to happen. Which left me with a dilemma: did I tell Cara her sister was going to be killed and watch her risk everything to save her, or did I keep it secret from her to protect her, and give her the freedom to leave?

CARA

ELEVEN

Middle of the night, and I felt it for the first time: a kick. It was like someone was knocking on the inside of my stomach, trying to push their way out. Hand on my belly, I felt a wave of love for the tiny being inside me, and more than ever I was compelled to try and protect them. A wrench in my stomach reminded me of how much I'd need to protect them from. The Saurians. Myla.

It was sometimes weird for me to think that Myla and I were sisters, so different were we. She'd always been very black and white about things – once she made up her mind, that was it. If she believed in something, she believed it 100 percent, and nothing could change that. Because of what happened to our mother, she believed that Ys were evil – they were to blame, so they had to be punished. She had no compassion for them whatsoever.

I saw things differently. I could always understand that the Ys were just as much victims as us. Yes, they could be dangerous, and yes, perhaps we should take care around them – but ultimately, I couldn't help but feel sorry for them.

I remember something Brown told me, early on in our relationship.

"Being a Y is a bit like ice-skating on a lake that you know has a weakness, but you don't know where. At any minute you could be plunged into the icy water, and you're powerless to stop it."

He made me realise how scary it must be. I couldn't hate anyone who lived in such fear.

If this baby were born a Y, my sister would want them enslaved, or worse. Stroking my tummy, it became suddenly clear that my child was more important to me than Myla, and I would do whatever was needed to keep it safe.

With the mission now only seven days away, training was becoming more and more intense. The official line was that we were going to attack and defeat the Saurians using skill, force and weaponry – the whole vaccine infection part was still only known to those right at the top. As far as everyone else was aware, the Ys who had volunteered were coming along as necessary helpers: the runners had intel on the whereabouts of nests and the hunters could feed the recruits. That hadn't stopped the speculation that they would be used as fighters, or even human shields. Luckily for Myla, there seemed to be no suspicion that they would be injected with what was effectively a poison and left to die.

If this got out, I wasn't sure what the consequences would be. Many citizens were too young to have really close ties to the Ys, which was perhaps why they stayed fairly passive despite Myla's strong stance. This was murder, though – a form of genocide, even. Myla was no longer controlling the Ys to keep us safe, but sacrificing them for 'the greater good'.

Whenever I thought back to her revelation about the plan, my heart plummeted. My sister, the monster. Where had my protective big sister gone? Had I lost her completely?

I'd calmed her in the past. A word, a look, could defuse her. Something had shifted between us, though: maybe I'd pulled back too far, got in too deep with Brown. Or maybe she had just floated further and further away from her humanity. I'd left her untethered and now she'd drifted beyond my reach.

I needed to find a way to drag her back, or let her go entirely. She could no longer be my priority.

*

I'd tried to see Brown the night his friend died. Whether he didn't hear me, or didn't want to, I'm not sure. I suspected he needed some time, to grieve for one thing, and to calm down after the way Myla spoke to him.

I was going to have to try again, though. It was only a week until the mission when we'd both be in danger. Despite my warning, Brown seemed determined to go. He'd been training with the Ys for weeks now, as they prepared to accompany our recruits. With Myla's plot a secret, they had no idea all this was pointless. If I didn't stop it, they would be dead before any fighting even began.

Because I couldn't let Myla take this step. Whatever had happened in our past, deliberately sacrificing Ys was not an option. I had a duty to my sister to close this door for her, because if she opened it, I'd never get her back.

I had a duty to Brown to keep him safe and ensure he became my equal.

Most of all, I had a duty to my unborn child – I would not let them grow up in a world like the one Myla wanted Galex to become.

*

Checking my appearance, I headed out into the city. I'd been absent from operations for long enough: I had to at least show my face. My top hung low and skimmed the shadow of my bump. If I were careful, and counting on no one taking much interest, I could get away with saying I was bloated, time of the month, etc. I grabbed a hoodie and wrapped it round me in case anyone thought to look closely.

Turning left to the training ground, I mentally catalogued the sights of Galex, my home up until this point in life. Whereas once it had been covered in debris and rubble, the streets were pretty tidy now. Parks had flowered, walls painted with bright murals and gathering places established. On warm days, the streets would be teeming with life, as people shared a drink and a chat. Today there was a cold wind though, and I was glad of the hoodie.

I heard the training ground before I saw it. The rhythmic thump of stick on stick, as the recruits practised hand-to-hand combat. The nerves settled in my stomach, unwilling to disappear: I considered how ineffective this would be against the strength of a Saurian. The best chance the recruits had was teamwork and persistence. If they could isolate the creatures, attack them one by one, then we might have a chance.

I was also struggling to think of ways Myla's vaccine plan could be thwarted. My choices seemed bleak – alert the Ys, and we'd be looking at a revolt. If I refused to go along with it, I felt pretty confident that Myla would find another way it could go ahead, probably with me losing control of the mission. If I wanted to protect Brown and try to save the rest of the Ys, Myla had to be clueless that anything was amiss. Even if she found out later, I suspected Brown's days would be numbered.

As things stood at the minute, I needed a way to save the Ys, not alert Myla and still give the recruits the best possible chance against the Saurians. I also had to decide how much to tell Brown. If he knew about the vaccine, he could put us all at risk. He would want to warn the others. He might not believe that I could find a way out of this. For now, I needed a way to keep him and the rest of the Ys on side so I could figure out the answer.

I hated having to keep him in the dark, but at this stage, it was for his own good. I needed time.

*

When I arrived at the training ground, Tyra bounced up to me.

"Hi Cara! We haven't seen you for ages! Are you okay?"

I smiled warmly at her, appreciative of her concern.

"I'm fine, thank you. Just run off my feet with all the planning and preparation for the mission."

Tyra rubbed her freckled nose, nodding. "It must be intense. Is there anything I can do to help?"

"Thank you, but all I need you to do at the minute is keep training. I'll need everybody to be at their best."

I didn't add, because I will not be at the forefront with you. Of course, I would be there, but I was planning a more managerial role, or some sort of responsibility that would avoid direct combat. I could no longer justify putting myself in extreme physical danger if I could possibly avoid it.

"You seen Ilana?" I asked.

Tyra pointed right. "Over there, working with the Ys." I heard the disdain in her voice – it caught me by surprise. I thought I'd had a bigger impact on her, on all the recruits, teaching them that respect went both ways.

"Thanks," I said, heading in that direction. I couldn't afford to pick a battle with her about it now.

Ilana was teaching a small group of about five Ys a formation which looked like a tactic to separate a Saurian and surround him. She saw me approach, said something to the trainees and came over.

"I was hoping I'd see you, today," she said, her dark hair sticking up in unruly angles. "We've not had much time to catch up."

The look she gave me suggested she knew I'd been avoiding her. To be fair, I thought, I'd been avoiding everyone. It had taken a while to get my head sorted, to decide what I wanted and to come up with a plan.

"I need to talk to you," I started, hoping she wasn't going to hold a grudge.

"I'm glad," she said. "I've been worried about you." I

realised I didn't need to worry. I'd misjudged her tone – it was concern rather than annoyance.

"Can we go somewhere private?" I asked. "Maybe the Park Centre."

"Great plan. There's that old fort there which will give us some shelter from this biting wind. I'm due a break anyway. So are these guys." She gestured to the Ys, still running drills. "I've worked them ragged this morning."

She called to them to pause and recharge, before we headed out of the training ground.

The Park Centre was a spacious green, with tarmacked paths and flower beds. It had always been a public area and was now less depressing, with regrowth and even some colour in the summer months. It still looked fairly sparse on a cloudy day though, so we approached what was known as the fort. It had once been some sort of café/gift shop, but all that remained were the foundations and half a wall. We plonked ourselves down against this, using it as a wind break.

"How are you feeling?" Ilana asked.

"Better than I was in terms of sickness, if that's what you mean. I must be around 20 weeks now, give or take. I'm still exhausted, but I think that's down to all the preparation."

"It's relentless, isn't it?" she agreed. "The recruits are nervous. They're worried they're going to be eaten alive."

"They should be nervous," I said. "We're asking a lot."

"Do you think they can handle it?" Ilana looked at me, her eyes concerned.

I shrugged. "I don't know. Has Myla told you the full plan?" I looked at her sideways, curious to see how she took it.

"You mean the vaccine? She has," Ilana answered quietly. "I'm struggling to process it."

"Me too," I added, relieved that she wasn't as gung-ho about it as my sister. "We can't let her do this. Whatever you think about Ys, deliberately poisoning them and leaving them for dead? As bait for the Saurians? I can't have that on my conscience. Not if I can do anything to stop it."

Ilana sighed. "That's what I wanted to talk to you about. I need to know what you're thinking of doing. You know, about the baby. And the father."

I held her gaze. "If I tell you, it could put you in danger."

"Cara, in a week's time I'll literally be fighting enormous lizard creatures. I think I'm going to be in danger no matter what."

"True," I laughed. "Okay. Well, the main priority is the baby. As in, me keeping the baby."

Ilana released her breath. "So, you've decided? You want to be a mother?"

Even as she said the words, I knew this was what I wanted more than anything.

"I do."

"In reality, what does that mean?" She asked the question gently. She realised what I was saying – to be a mother, to keep this baby – I couldn't be in Galex. Not the way it was currently set up.

"I'm not coming back from the mission." Once I'd spoken the words, it suddenly seemed so real. I would be leaving behind everything I knew, my sister and my friends. Was I strong enough? I had to be, I realised, for my child.

"And Brown? Have you thought about him?"

"I want him to come with me. I need to speak to him – I haven't ironed out the details yet. I just know we're in this together and we owe it to our baby to at least try to be together."

Ilana nodded thoughtfully. "I guessed you'd say this," she admitted. "So, I've been doing some digging of my own, into the so-called vaccine."

My ears pricked up. I needed a plan – a way to change the direction of the mission.

"I went down to the science lab to find out how and when we were meant to be injecting the Ys with the vaccine. Turns out, it takes about two days before death occurs, meaning it's most sensible to inject them outside the city walls, after the first night camping out. I think the idea is to sell it as some sort of vitamin boost."

"I'm not sure that sounds entirely convincing, given the way they've been treated. 'Hey, we've acted like you're disposable for years, but here, have some vitamins to keep you healthy!' Who are they planning on having actually administer the injections?" I asked, horrified. If it were the recruits, they could be unwittingly giving a death sentence to anyone they injected.

Ilana must have read my mind. "I know, I was worried about the implications for the recruits too, so I offered to inject the vaccine myself."

"Do you think you can handle that?" I asked, knowing I'd struggle myself. I was secretly glad she'd taken this on though – I didn't think I'd be able to volunteer myself, and if Myla had asked me, this would have been a sure-fire way to raise her suspicions.

She sighed. "I don't know. I wanted to talk to you about it."

"If there's any way we can disobey Myla, you mean?"

"Well, yeah. Or say it didn't work."

I thought about it.

"Possibly. The worry is we're still expected to kill all the Saurian threat we come across. How can we ensure we do that without the vaccine plan?"

"I don't know. I do know I can't offer the Ys up the way Myla wants us to. Who are we to make such life or death decisions? Plus, we were planning to attack before this vaccine became part of the plan."

"Well, we've trained the recruits hard, they can handle themselves." My voice sounded confident, but I felt my stomach drop. Had we done enough? Were they ready?

Again, Ilana seemed to put my thoughts into words.

"Wouldn't it be great to give them a head start, though? Let them tackle the nest, sure, but one where the inhabitants weren't at full fitness."

She had a point. The thought of the recruits fighting and dying … Versus the thought of them winning with ease against half-dead Saurians. It was a compelling mental image.

I steeled myself, shaking my brain free from these imaginings. Thinking of Brown and the baby, thinking of the kind of person I wanted to be, I replied, "In theory, of course. If it didn't mean the sacrifice of innocent Ys. Regardless, I need to make sure Brown is safe."

Business-like, Ilana continued. "Right. I thought as much. Which is why I asked the scientists about an antidote."

"For the vaccine?"

She nodded. "Yup. And that's the good part. We have plenty of it." She smiled.

"How do you mean?"

"It's us. Xs. Our blood has antibodies that fight the virus – that's why we're immune to the serious effects. Inject our antibodies into a Y and it helps their bodies to fight against the impact of the vaccine."

"Well, that is good news," I responded, processing her words. "It means that even if we have to go through with the injections to avoid raising suspicions, we have a means to reverse the vaccine. It leaves her with a much less powerful weapon against the Ys too."

Still thinking, I added, "Does it help much with our attack? If we don't inject the Ys, or if we do and then cure them, we're still no better off against the Saurians."

"I may have an answer," Ilana countered. "If it works, we should be able to give everyone on the mission a fighting chance of survival."

*

I left Ilana as she headed back to the training ground, feeling much clearer and more secure now she had offered up a solution, albeit a risky one. If Brown insisted on coming on the mission, at least I could do something to try and keep him safe until we could make our getaway. My priority now was to make him talk to me, to tell him how sorry I was about Blue, and to give him hope that we could leave Galex and be together. It was all I wanted: a family. If it meant a difficult life, on the road, dodging danger, I'd take it. I was no longer safe if I stayed, anyway – Myla would see to that the minute we undermined her plans. I just had to get through the next week and then not look back.

MYLA

TWELVE

I knew when Gloria told us she wanted Cara to be left in charge of the city that I had to stop that from happening. It was my job to keep Cara safe, and that meant protecting her from her own weakness. Her weakness being human kindness, of course. She has too much of it in her, particularly when it comes to Ys. I felt like I was honouring Mum's memory by making sure she didn't give in to her softer impulses.

I'd tried to keep her away from anything that could weaken her. Once, a stray dog had got into the city, God knows how with the size of the walls. It latched onto Cara, following her everywhere. She fed it, played with it, cuddled it at night. I felt a stab of envy when I felt she might prefer the mutt to me, her own sister. But more than that, this pet made her vulnerable. She would put its needs before her own.

I solved that problem fairly easily. I lured the dog away one evening, took it to the edge of the city. Once it could see a way out, I pelted it with stones. Many of them hit their target. The creature took a while to get the hint: I'm fairly sure it was lame by the time it finally realised Cara wasn't going to come and rescue it. Eventually it hobbled off, and thankfully it had the good sense not to return. Either that, or it met its end in some other way. Cara cried for days when she realised it'd gone.

This Y, though. I suspected he would cause me a far bigger headache. I'd need to be careful: the dog was one thing. Destroying someone she loved? That was a different matter. This relationship couldn't continue though. He was dangerous; they all were. Plus, he was taking her from me. She seemed further away, somehow.

I could tell she disapproved of the Y vaccine plan. Obviously she would want to protect this Brown, to stop him from being given the injection. I'd need to make sure I had eyes on the mission so that her failure could be overturned. Making his death seem like an accident would also be beneficial: at least that way, she couldn't blame me. She would need me with him gone, and I'd be her protector again.

A knock at the door brought the pathetic Tyra in. I could tell instantly she had something good for me. She was almost vibrating, so excited was she. I inwardly sneered at her, so easy was she to manipulate. To betray her mentor in this way, believing she was helping! I could imagine her guilt-ridden expression if she ever realised I'd been using her for my own gain.

I dispensed with any preamble. "What have you got for me?"

Quivering, she gave me more than I could have hoped for. "She's pregnant!" This news burst out of her, as if she couldn't hold it in.

For a moment, I was floored. Truly shocked. Quickly, I recovered myself. "I see," I said, as calmly as I could. I paused, digesting this news. Pregnant!

"I followed Cara and Ilana to the fort: they went there for a private chat," Tyra continued breathlessly. "I hid out of sight behind the wall, but could hear everything clearly." She hesitated, perhaps expecting a pat on the back for her ingenuity. I stayed silent, until she stumblingly carried on.

"Ilana already knew about it, she was asking how Cara felt. She said she wants to keep the baby – she's planning on running away, on not coming back to Galex after the mission! She wants to make a life with that runner."

This hit like a stab in the gut. I couldn't let go of Cara – no matter how angry I was that she was lying to me, that she'd gone behind my back. I *needed* her here.

"What else did she say?" I tried to keep my voice steady, despite feeling like my whole body was shaking.

"They talked about a vaccine that kills the Ys. Is that part of the mission?"

This was becoming tricky. Even though she wasn't the brightest tool in the box, if Tyra opened her mouth about the plan to anyone, she could make my position very difficult.

"What exactly was said?" I tried simply deflecting her question as much as possible.

"They discussed using the antibodies in X blood to reverse the effects of the vaccine. Ilana offered to collect blood samples from all the recruits in advance to take with them. That's all I heard – I had to leave my hiding spot with the approach of some citizens." Tyra's glum face told me she felt deflated at the thought of Cara leaving.

She wasn't the only one. This felt like such a betrayal. After the years I'd spent looking out for her, she would be prepared to leave me here without even a goodbye. All for a Y.

It also sounded like she might be planning to derail my vaccine plan. This, on its own, wasn't the end of the world – it would mean a few more Ys to deal with and would probably mean more dead recruits when they attacked the nest. That guilt would have to be on Cara – I'd wanted to give them the best possible chance for survival. If she was prioritising Ys, it would only help my cause when they returned. I'd be able to use any deaths of Xs against them.

My priority was to stop her leaving. I needed a way to make sure she'd come back from this mission.

"So, what next?" Tyra's voice interrupted my musings. I'd been worried she would be a liability, but I could see a role for her now.

"Now listen to me," I said sternly, well aware of the steel running through my voice. Tyra paled under my stare. "You say nothing about anything you've heard, or think you know, ever. If I hear you've opened your mouth to anyone, I will cut you down myself."

The look in her eyes told me she believed me.

"Consider yourself my eyes and ears on the mission. Your priority is to get Cara back here after the mission. It seems to me that removing her temptation is the answer. Under no circumstances must you allow Brown to survive."

"Do you mean, kill him myself?" She gulped, clearly not keen on the direction this was taking.

"Whatever it takes. Stop Cara saving him, stab him, I don't

care. I just need him gone. For Cara's sake," I added lamely.

She nodded, biting her lip in worry. "Will Cara know I did it?"

Aha. This was what she was afraid of – losing the respect of her idol.

"Definitely not," I lied easily. "Cover your tracks. I'm sure a smart girl like you can manage that."

A bit of flattery never hurt to help you get what you wanted.

"And remember – when Cara comes to her senses, she'll thank you anyway. You'll be her hero, for saving her."

This seemed to swing it.

"And the baby?"

I needed Tyra gone so I could think things through more clearly. This blasted baby was a complication. "I'd imagine with Brown out of the picture she'll realise what needs to be done." I didn't elaborate on my fear that if she wanted to be a proper mother, she'd realise Galex wasn't the place for that. I sensed that a child would always trump a sister in the loyalty stakes.

"What if I can't get her to come back? Even without the Y?"

"Don't worry," I answered, keeping my tone neutral. "I'll make sure I have a back-up plan in place."

BROWN

THIRTEEN

"Everything's now in motion," Eeyore announced smugly. "We've built up quite a following – not surprising given how much we've had to put up with over the last few years." He was sporting a black eye and a thick lip which I assumed came courtesy of Myla.

"It looks like we'll have more than enough volunteers to overthrow things here, especially with the majority of the recruits out of the way."

He turned to 6 and me. "You still okay to keep them busy?"

6 nodded. "Yup. We reckon a fair few will be killed fighting the Saurians anyway. I'm not sure they really understand what they're walking into." His face hardened, and I could tell he was thinking back to the night we saw our friends killed. "Orange swiped some sleeping pills from the lab. The idea is to lace their water with it after the worst of the fighting is over. Not much, just a tiny dosage, really. Should leave them dopey, and not keen to rush back."

Eeyore inclined his head, clearly pleased with what he

heard. "Sounds good. You'll just have to be careful – we need you alive. Don't let them throw you to the Saurians." He laughed to show he was joking, but 6 and I stayed uncomfortably quiet. It was a possibility that had crossed our minds – that if things got bad, we'd be the first ones sacrificed. I knew Cara would protect me, but 6 had no such reassurance.

"In all seriousness, you might be best served leaving them to it – find somewhere to hide out and wait until the worst is over."

6 and I looked at each other. Eeyore's suggestion felt … cowardly. We might not be as well trained, but leaving the recruits to face the creatures whilst we hid? It didn't sit right with me, and from his eye contact, I think 6 felt the same. The Saurians were a common enemy. And, after what we saw on the last mission, an evolving one. Yes, they were dangerous and yes, I was terrified. But I wouldn't let Cara face them without me there.

"And you're still sorted with your side?" He addressed me directly now.

"I think so," I answered, sounding more confident than I felt. "While the others are out for the count, I'll take Cara and get a head start. 6 will tell the others that we left early as she was keen to get back and give Myla the good news."

"Of course, your side of this all rests on the assumption that our army can overpower the Saurians. But either way, we should still be able to take over the city. In a way," he added coolly, his dark eyes glittering, "the fewer that return the better. They'll be the tougher ones to overpower."

He said it so calmly, it took a minute for me to realise he was basically saying he didn't care if the Xs lived or died.

Either that, or he was kind of hoping we'd slaughter any surviving recruits in their sleep, to save them extra hassle. The similarity between his thinking and Myla's was not lost on me. My doubts about this rebellion resurfaced – it really would be exchanging one dictatorship for another.

At this stage though, I had to keep a step back. Cara and the baby were the most important things now. Keeping them safe was my priority, not saving the world. With a bit of luck, Cara and I would be halfway to Amex before anyone even realised we were missing.

"Understood," I replied, non-committally.

He continued. "Things are really moving forward now. With our numbers, we should be able to get to Myla before she realises what's happening. We've even managed to swipe a few weapons. They're not great, but they should give us the drop on the few who're left behind to protect her."

Looking at his face, I could imagine the strength of feeling behind his words and realised this was probably echoed across the rest of the group. I supposed I'd been so caught up with Cara I hadn't even realised how deep this hatred went. Myla didn't see us as human, so I guess I could understand the fact that this feeling ran the other way too. Yes, I found it hard being treated like a second-class citizen, but I think my role as a runner at least gave me time out and some freedom away from the city. If I didn't have that, or didn't have Cara treating me as an equal, I'd probably be as desperate as these guys. I'd also probably want to destroy the monster who threatened my life every day.

"Is there a back-up plan?" Red asked, a worry line creasing his forehead, causing his eyebrows to beetle together. "I mean, what if we don't kill her? What if Myla and the Xs still manage to win?"

Eeyore took a second to gather himself before speaking. "If that happens, if we fail – we're all dead. She won't let us get away with it." He paused again, watching the implications of this sink in. "Which is why we have to get it right. There won't be a second chance."

*

I spent the afternoon at the training ground, preparing for the mission. We'd all left the meeting feeling fairly despondent: if there was even a slim chance of failure, we were taking a massive risk. Even though I was planning on disappearing, I couldn't stand the thought of my friends being murdered. I felt torn again: torn between my instinct to protect my friends, and my instinct to protect Cara. If I could cut myself in two to help both, I would. As it was, I'd have to put my faith in the strength and determination of the Ys to pull through.

I hoped Eeyore and the other instigators of this coup weren't underestimating Myla. She was wily and ruthless – it wouldn't surprise me if she had something up her sleeve in the event of an ambush – I know I would if I was her. I suppose they were just hoping she'd be distracted, with so much riding on the mission. If she managed to defeat the Saurians, she'd be hailed a true hero.

I glimpsed Cara when she came to collect her friend, Ilana. She looked glowing – her hair shone and her cheeks were rosy. I could just make out the slight curve of her stomach underneath a hooded top. Ice twisted in my gut.

Did I see it because I was looking for a bump, or would other people notice too?

Nobody gave her a second glance, though, so intent were they on their training. The air felt tense; such a lot was at stake for those going.

They held the future of Galex and possibly the human race in their hands.

Cara and I hadn't really spoken since Blue had died, but with the mission fast approaching I knew we needed to talk. I hoped she was thinking along the same lines as me – escape seemed our only option if we wanted to be together. Looking at her now, she seemed vulnerable for the first time, as she crossed her arms over her tummy. As she waited, I caught her eye, gave her a half wink before turning back to training. I could only hope she saw and took it as a sign to come over tonight.

*

The stones woke me around one a.m. I think I'd only been half asleep, keeping one ear open for her, because I was up and out quicker than ever. Finding her waiting for me at the bottom corner of the garden, I went straight up and folded her into a huge hug. I closed my eyes. Even with everything on my mind, this made me feel warm and protected.

"The bump is starting to show! Can I touch it?"

"Of course!" She laughed, guiding my hand down. "If you're lucky, you'll feel a little kick."

Her stomach felt smooth and taut. "Wow," I breathed. "Can you believe we made a baby?"

Her eyes twinkled. "Not really. It still doesn't feel real most of the time."

Thud. A tiny impulse pressed against my hand.

"I felt it!" I gasped, feeling a burst of love for the unborn child.

"It's amazing, isn't it? Blob is very active in the evenings."

"Blob?" I asked, loving the nickname.

"Blob," Cara repeated, smiling. "Right now, this baby's only about half cooked – they're not fully formed yet."

"We might have to think of a better name eventually."

She laughed. I was glad it was easy between us again. Cara must have been thinking the same thing because she said, "I was worried about you. After your friend …" She paused, and I hung my head, willing the image of Blue to go away. "I was worried you wouldn't want to see me anymore."

I took her hand. "I'll always want to see you, Cara. I love you. It's just hard sometimes. You know," I finished lamely.

"I do know," she replied. "It's hard for me too. I know it's better for me," she added quickly, before I could protest. "But it's still difficult. We can't be together, and I don't agree with the way Myla runs things. To be honest, I'm worried I've lost her already. Plus, this baby has made it impossible for me."

"So –" we both spoke at once. Giggling, I told Cara to go first.

"So – I've an idea. About the mission." She looked at me, gauging my reaction.

"I have an idea too – what's the betting we've both got the same idea?"

"Is your idea to run away and make a life elsewhere?" Cara asked cheekily.

"Yup. Yours too?"

"Uh huh. Great minds, hey?" We chuckled.

"I suppose we don't have many options. It seems the only way we can stay together and raise our child."

Our child. I loved hearing her say this.

"I'm just glad we're on the same page. I thought with your sister being here, and her becoming an aunt – you might want to stay, try and make things work."

Cara grasped my hands tight. "I know Myla. Nothing, not a baby, not anything, will change her mind. I'd have to give the baby up, and I can't do that. I'd also have to give you up too. And I won't."

I sighed deeply. "I'm glad. Relieved. I think we have a real shot at a new life."

"Where we'll end up, I've no idea." Her hands moved protectively to her belly.

"Well, I've got an idea of the where. I'm not saying the journey won't be dangerous, but if we make it, and it's what I think – we've got a real chance of making a great life together."

Cara looked at me questioningly, hope reflecting from her eyes. "So? Tell me!" she demanded eagerly.

"I heard about this place. Another City. It's called Amex –"

"Wait," she interrupted. "That rings a bell."

"Gloria, the leader before Myla – she was leading an expedition there."

"Yes!" Cara exclaimed, eyes shining. "I remember. I knew I recognised the name. Myla dismissed it as a fairy-tale,

175

so any plans to try and reach Amex again were abandoned."

"I'm not surprised she'd say that," I continued. "By all accounts, it's a hugely different society from Galex. It's more equal, with the hope of a cure for the Epidemic." At this, Cara seemed to bristle.

"Really? That sounds almost too good to be true," she said sceptically.

Now it was my turn to bristle. "I can't promise what it'll actually be like. But it's worth a try, surely? I even have a map – look!" I grabbed the now severely creased scrap of paper from my back pocket and smoothed it out for her to see. She snatched it from me, her nose pressed close. I realised how childlike the symbols looked, but that despite this, it was a clear map with landmarks and a compass.

"Where on earth did you get this from?" Cara asked slowly.

"A crazy man who lives like a hermit in the library," I shrugged nonchalantly. This broke the tension and she laughed, as I'd known she would.

"O-kay then," she studied the map further. "I mean, it could be accurate. I'm not going to bet my life on it, but I suppose it's better than nothing." She stopped short and gasped, grabbing my hand and placing it on her tummy.

"I felt it!" That warm feeling returned, and I knew we were doing the right thing.

About half an hour later, when Cara was leaving, she said, "I just hope Myla doesn't find out. I need her to be in the dark on this. No matter what she is, she thinks she needs me. She can't know I'm leaving. She'd stop at nothing to keep me here."

I watched her go, the words, 'If she's still alive', dying in my throat. I'd seen her excitement. I'd seen how much she needed to keep the baby, to get away.

I couldn't let her risk her happiness for her sister.

FOURTEEN

The few days leading up to the mission passed swiftly, a blur of training and preparing. Rumbling in the background was the plot against Myla, gaining momentum every day. From the whisperings, huddles in corners and general air of anticipation, I guessed most of the Ys were in on it. They'd have to keep it together until we'd all left: I wouldn't fancy their chances against a large group of highly trained recruits. Once they were out of the city, though – I was seriously starting to doubt Myla's chances.

I'd had a couple of sleepless nights now, wrestling with bad dreams. Someone was chasing me, or hunting me really. I kept running until my lungs felt on the verge of collapse. I'd end up cornered by a slobbering, drooling Saurian, who at the last minute changed into Cara. I always woke up just at the moment she was about to attack me.

It didn't take a genius to work out that I was feeling guilty about lying to her. Well, not lying exactly, but keeping information from her. About five times every day I resolved to tell her – I owed her the truth, she had a right to know her sister was in danger, all that stuff. At the last minute though, I chickened out. The thought of me and her on the road, the thought of being able to hold my baby – the image of this potential future made me keep my mouth shut. I needed us away from Myla's poison, whether she was Cara's sister or not.

Myla hadn't helped the situation by making her presence felt at the training ground. For a few days now, it had almost felt like she was targeting me. Every time we ran drills, she was on hand to make my group go again. When she wanted to show the recruits a choke hold, I was the volunteer she picked to practise on. I felt other eyes on me too. The recruit Tyra seemed unusually interested in my comings and goings. I would have mentioned it to Cara, but I'd seen how much this younger girl looked up to her – I didn't doubt that she'd be able to keep her in line.

All this left me with a feeling of dread, though; a sense that something was going on and things weren't quite as they seemed. It felt like the moment before a storm – everyone was on edge and expecting destruction. It got so I was counting down the hours until we left Galex; at least outside the city I had a chance of freedom.

*

When the day of the mission was finally upon us, I felt only relief, regardless of the danger facing us. It felt like the end of an era – I wouldn't see Galex again, wouldn't be identified as a number, rather than as a human. Imagining what could be,

I felt giddy, an excitement I'd not experienced since being a kid. I even welcomed the unknown: anything, I reasoned, would be better if it involved freedom.

Every so often my elation would be punctured by the realisation that the pay off for this freedom was that we'd be part of an attack on the Saurians. Strangely, this didn't particularly alarm me, though – or at least, not as much as a future without Cara did. If I could just protect her and the baby, I'd face a million Saurians.

There were only five runners and five hunters in the end, and six times as many Xs. We must have been a formidable sight, filing out the city gates, cheered on by the community. Hopes were high: with the Saurian threat gone, people were looking forward to spreading their wings, to more space. A possible future outside the city. I wished them well – I sincerely hoped it worked out. If Myla were gone, it would certainly be a more realistic proposition.

We trekked miles the first day following Brown 10, nicknamed Scooter on account of his speed, making our way to a large nest discovered a few months ago. There were four sites to attack: it had been decided to start with the biggest. This didn't make a lot of sense to me – I'd have thought going for the smallest first would have been less risky and give them a better idea of how they'd cope against the Saurians. I'm not military minded though, so what did I know?

Going at a steady pace, the nest was just under a three-day journey away, meaning there'd be two nights spent camping out under the stars. The Ys were strangely upbeat: perhaps buoyed up by the thought of the rebellion back home, the night sky seemed a fitting backdrop to a hopeful time.

We set up our tents a short way from the Xs – we didn't want to be on top of them, but neither did we want to be miles away. They had the weapons after all, and there were plenty of dangers way out here. Despite no known nests nearby, I didn't fancy meeting one of the newly evolved, more intelligent Saurians on my own.

Cara and I had already agreed it was safest to ignore each other, at least in the beginning. Once the large nest had been defeated, we'd go. She wanted to make sure her recruits could handle themselves before disappearing. I was less sure – I wanted her as far away from the danger as possible. I couldn't persuade her though, and I suppose in her shoes I'd be wanting to do the same. I had made her promise to stay out of the direct combat, and I was prepared to drag her back if she looked like throwing herself into it.

"Don't worry," she'd said. "My priorities have definitely shifted. I won't risk it. I'll find a safe spot with my spear and help out from a distance if I'm needed." The determined look in her eyes told me I could believe her.

The first evening passed without incident. We sat around a fire, ate well and laughed. It was almost like being on holiday. I enjoyed the warmth of the flames on my face and felt at peace for the first time in a long time.

"Do you think they've done it yet?" 6 whispered, referring to the plot against Myla.

"I doubt it," I muttered. "I think they were planning to wait a day or two to take stock, be sure about how many recruits remained, see what sort of pattern the Boss got into. With only one shot at this, they wanted to be as well prepared as possible, making sure they knew her routines."

"You're probably right," he whispered back. "Just think – when we go back, everything will be different."

For his sake, and for the sake of the rest of the Ys, I hoped he was right. A shadow of guilt gnawed at my insides though, as I thought about Cara's reaction to the death of her sister.

*

The sun rose early, waking a nearby cuckoo for a dawn chorus. I couldn't resent the early alarm clock – it felt like a long time since a bird had serenaded me in the morning. Unzipping my tent, I breathed in the fresh, cool air, letting it fill my lungs. I felt … alive. I put it down to the power of hope, something which had been missing for a long time.

As the rest of the camp woke up and started bustling around, washing and cooking breakfast, I tried to keep an eye on Cara. She looked tired and pale. I suspected that the mission was weighing heavily on her mind. As would be the fact she'd left her sister behind for good. Guilt was a funny thing: even though she was doing what was best for the baby and for me, I knew she'd feel she was letting the recruits down. And strangely, she'd feel guilty for abandoning Myla. They had a blood tie, and a shared history. These things can be hard to let go of – another reminder that I needed to keep the planned assassination from her. I couldn't risk her letting a tug of loyalty draw her back.

I did notice that I wasn't the only one keeping a close watch on her. Tyra barely took her eyes off her; they followed her every movement. It was when she hopped up to help Cara lift a heavy-looking backpack that I felt a cold trickle down my spine. From the way she'd jumped to protect her, I guessed that she also knew Cara's secret.

*

"Have you told Tyra?" I hissed at Cara, when I crossed paths with her as we were packing up to go about half an hour later.

"Of course not! Why?" she whispered back, continuing to wash out her pots.

I bent to tie my shoelace, buying me a few more seconds near her. "From the way she's been looking at you, I think she knows. About the baby," I added, barely audibly.

"She can't. She'd have said," Cara replied, but her tone was doubtful.

"Just be careful," I shot back. "Don't let your guard down."

"I won't," she answered, putting her pots away and lifting on her rucksack. "I promise."

*

Before we set off, something was happening. The Ys were forming a sort of line and waiting around, while Ilana fiddled about with something. She'd set up what looked like a mini-lab – a folding chair for the patient and a small table holding various boxes. I kept an eye on the front of the queue from my vantage point at the back. Ilana sat each person down, rolled their t-shirt sleeve up to expose the upper arm and injected them with something.

I frowned. This didn't feel good. What would they be injecting us with? I scoured around, to see if the Xs had a similar area set up where they were getting the same treatment. There was none. A feeling of unease crept over me: why had Cara not said anything about this?

By the time I'd reached the front, I'd worked myself up. I kept looking round wildly for Cara, but she was nowhere to be seen.

"What's going on?" I demanded.

Ilana looked uncomfortable. "Just a vitamin shot," she replied, busy prepping my needle. Her eyes were intent on her work, meaning she could easily avoid eye contact. "You'll hardly feel it."

"How come it's only for the Ys?"

"We all had ours before the mission. It was easier to get them out the way," she added lamely. I could tell she was lying. Finally, I caught sight of Cara, and decided I had to break protocol: I had to know what this was, or at least know if it was safe. I was pretty pissed off, too: she should have warned me about this, no matter how innocent it was. It felt like another reminder of how much power the Xs, including her, still had over me.

"Excuse me!" I called.

Doing a double take, Cara realised I was addressing her and walked over. She looked faintly surprised – I realised it was the first time I'd spoken openly to her in front of other people.

"What's the problem?" she answered brusquely.

"These jabs – do we really have to have them?"

"They're for your own good," she answered quickly.

"Why, you scared of a little needle?" I knew the mocking voice she had adopted was intended to make me look small – it was sensible, she had to play her part until we were ready to leave.

"No. Just asking. How do we know they're safe? For all we know, you could be poisoning us."

"Relax. We're going to need all the bodies we can get when we ambush the Saurians. Why would we kill off a chunk of our resources? It wouldn't make any sense." She herded the nearby Ys towards Ilana, getting them into the line. Once they were out of earshot, she whispered, "You'll have to trust me. You know I wouldn't do anything to harm you."

After only a tiny pause, I did as I was told. It still didn't feel right, but I had to trust Cara.

I barely flinched as the needle pierced my flesh.

*

It was another long walk. The runners still stayed up front, but we kept a slow pace so as not to lose the group. An unspoken agreement told us it was sensible to preserve our energy for the coming days. The weather was less kind today, and intermittent showers blighted our trek. I didn't really mind, though – in fact, the cool rain was preferable to a baking sun. Even though we didn't camp up again until early evening, I felt fairly refreshed, with the weariness that usually seeped through my bones after a long journey absent.

Camp was set up swiftly and Cara assumed authority naturally, strategically placing guards at each perimeter and allocating additional recruits to undertake constant patrols.

Sitting around the fire in the evening, I kept absent-mindedly scratching the injection point. I'd noticed other Ys doing it to. A shadow flickered across my mind again – had it really been as innocent as a vitamin boost? And why would Cara lie to me if it was something else?

"What d'you reckon to the jabs we got given?" I asked 6 as dusk fell, and the orange sun burnt onto the land.

He shrugged, gnawing scraps of meat clinging to the bone of a jackdaw the hunters had brought down.

"Dunno. Vitamins or something? Perhaps they're worried we'll all turn into Saurians and give them another nest to worry about."

He was joking, but nonetheless, his words got me thinking. What if the injections were something to do with the Saurians? An idea pinged into my mind, setting my heart rate off.

"What if," I paused, realising that what I was about to say sounded pretty insane. "I mean, you don't think – could they have found a vaccine? For the Epidemic?"

6 chewed thoughtfully, wiping meat juice from his stubbly chin. "Why wouldn't they tell us about that? You'd think the Boss would've been boasting about how clever they were."

"True," I felt deflated. Then I rallied. "What if they want to test the vaccine? Maybe they think if we come into close contact with a mutation, we might still mutate ourselves. Maybe this mission is actually about testing the vaccine!" In my excitement I'd accidentally raised my voice. After some curious glances from the nearby Xs, I toned the volume way down. "That would explain why we were brought along." And, I added silently, why Cara had let the injections go ahead.

"Maybe," 6 continued to pick tiny flecks of meat from the pile of bones that now lay in front of him. "Seems a bit risky though. Take a load of Ys to a load of Saurians to see if they mutate. What happens if we do transform? They could be seriously outnumbered then."

"And," he added, sucking the remaining juice from his fingers, "as if the Boss would approve a plan where things worked out for us."

He had a point.

"I guess," I conceded, defeated for now. I was on to something, though, I was sure of it. I may not quite have got it yet, but I would, I was certain. I was also certain that Cara knew the truth. I now just had to get her alone so I could find out exactly what was going on.

*

Once the sun had dipped below the horizon, the stars cast a greyish gloom over our camp. We were still a fair distance from the nest, so a final half day of travel was planned, giving us plenty of time to recuperate and get a full night's rest before a morning attack, when the Saurians would be at their weakest.

Out here, so far from Galex, the atmosphere was completely different. Although we kept separate from the Xs, the boundaries between us didn't seem as pronounced. They sat around their fire, just as we sat around ours. We shared the captured food. We shared the water supply. We'd even helped each other pitch tents. A glimmer of a life that could be.

So, when one of the recruits started to sing, we all listened in and enjoyed her gentle, but strangely commanding voice.

Shame on me for lovin' you,
It's all that I can ever do.
I lost myself somewhere down the line,
But without me you say you'd be just fine,
I can't stop how I feel in my heart,
I'd rather die than see us part.

Listening to the melancholy lyrics, staring into the burnished orange flames, I could have been anywhere. In that moment, there was no virus, no Saurians, no divisions. All I could see in my mind was Cara, growing our child. I understood I'd do anything to protect her – I'd die rather than see her hurt.

I was so in the moment, lost in my thoughts, that what happened next came as a complete shock.

*

Looking back, we should've been ready for it. We'd all let our guard down, focusing as we were on the planned attack. We'd allowed ourselves to feel relatively safe, what with the guards and patrols set up by Cara. With no nest nearby, we had thought this was enough.

The attack, when it came, took us by surprise and acted as another reminder that these beasts were steadily evolving into an even more formidable enemy.

It happened in an instant. One minute, we were sat drinking hot tea, and enjoying the singing. The next, two full grown Saurians plunged into our camp, hissing and roaring.

Their greenish scales twinkled in the firelight, and for a minute my brain still didn't register the full danger we were in. They looked magnificent: muscular, strong piston legs, pumping closer. Claws drawn, teeth snarling, they made for the recruits' area first.

One of the beasts went straight for the singer. With what seemed like ridiculous ease, it grabbed her up and shook her, as if she was a doll. Next, it smashed her face down on the earth. Again, and again. She stopped shrieking and went deadly still the second time her head hit the gravel. Not giving up, the beast continued to maul her before taking its prey and retreating. The rest of the recruits scurried around quickly, grabbing up weapons, trying not to give in to panic. I realised this was probably the first time they'd ever witnessed a Saurian attack outside the controlled environment of the training ground.

"Eleanor, Masha, Summer, after it! We need it brought down; we can't risk a second attack. Callie, Becka, Molly, Jet – provide back up!"

"Brown – can the Ys help too?" I nodded, giving 6 and Scooter the nudge – they were on their feet, all ready to go, clearly keen to help defeat the monster.

"The weapon trunk's there by the fire!"

Cara was so busy desperately shouting orders, trying to organise her troops to rally after this surprise attack, that she took her eye off the second Saurian. With red eyes flashing, it batted off the few brave recruits who'd already started to strike back and turned its attention to Cara. From the distance between us, I could only watch in horror as it sprang at her.

CARA

FIFTEEN

It was on me before I even had a chance to think. With a snarl, the beast bounded towards me, knocking me flat. I could do nothing but lay there quivering, as saliva dripped onto my chest. I gave up, silently praying for a quick, pain-free death. Brown flashed through my mind – I wished I'd had the chance to say goodbye and tell him I loved him. Hopeless though it was, my hands instinctively went to my stomach in a futile attempt to protect the baby. An agonising screech pierced the air as I found my voice to express my fear.

The Saurian's red-rimmed eyes stared vacantly down as it raised an arm ready to strike, its silver claws glistening with a bluish venom. I braced myself. In that moment though, something flashed in between us. Screaming, I could just make out Tyra in a blur of movement, as she sprinted up and launched herself at the creature, sinking a thin blade into its neck. The creature shrieked in pain and slashed wildly, catching Tyra square across the chest. I watched as blooms of red spread down her body, her mouth an open O as she flew back about ten feet, propelled by the strength of the impact. Suddenly, my instincts kicked in, and I scrabbled to turn onto my knees, my feet and started to run. By now other recruits had borne down on the Saurian, weakened by Tyra's fatal blow. A severed artery seemed to account for the oozing blood, a gloopy, thick substance which began to pool on the gravel. With a final roar, and a last attempt to swipe at a victim, the lizard slumped to the ground, still at last.

Heart pounding, I dashed over to Tyra, who was crumpled into an S shape. I could see the wounds on her chest were tinged with the dreaded blue: the venom would be too far in her bloodstream for us to save her now. All I could do was to make her last few moments as comfortable as possible.

Cradling her head, I soothed her with gentle words and stroked her hair, tears pricking my eyes. It was so unfair! She was brave, strong and loyal. A few months ago, I'd have gladly traded places with her. Now, I needed to stay alive for the sake of the baby. This didn't stop me feeling guilty that she had sacrificed her life for mine.

"I'm so sorry, Tyra," I wept. "You are my hero; you saved my life." I bent to kiss her clammy forehead. Thick cardinal blood soaked her top, staining my fingers as I pressed futilely on her wound.

She looked at me through hooded eyes. "No, you're my hero," she croaked hoarsely. "I had to protect you and … and your baby." I looked into her open face, so guileless. I saw her joy at my happy news and my heart went out to her.

"You knew?" I said.

She nodded weakly. "I have to confess. I've been spying on you. I told Myla," her breathing grew more laboured. My heart seemed to stop.

"I'm sorry," she continued, despite the effort it was taking. "I thought I was doing the right thing, I only wanted to protect you. But when she told me I had to kill the father and do anything to get you back to Galex … I knew I'd betrayed you. She wasn't thinking about your happiness." A solitary tear ran down her face. "I thought she was trying to protect you as well, but I think it's gone past that. Now, it's just about control."

I carried on stroking her face. "Don't worry," I soothed, "I forgive you. I know you will have had the best intentions towards me. Now just relax, I'm here, I won't leave you."

"Is everyone else safe?" Tyra asked, still more concerned with the safety of others than herself. I looked up to see the recruits I'd sent after the Saurian that fled return, giving me a grim thumbs up to signal they'd defeated it.

"We're all fine, the second Saurian has been brought down, and you single-handedly took care of the first." I smiled down at her, noticing her eyes becoming cloudy. It wouldn't be long now. "You can rest now."

She sighed, a rattling breath escaping her broken body. "Don't go back," she whispered. "Make a new life away from her. I've seen the way he looks at you. He'll protect you when I'm gone."

I couldn't stop the tears now. Bending to kiss her, I whispered "Ssh. Let me look after you now, my darling." Her eyes flickered. Her breath weakened. Within minutes, she was gone.

*

I can't remember much about the next few hours. I know I sat weeping next to Tyra's body for some time. Brown sat with me, keeping a distance at first, but soon he came closer and held my hand. I no longer cared what the others felt – I wasn't even sure it mattered anymore.

I cried for Tyra, I cried for Leia, the recruit who'd been killed by the first Saurian; I cried for our baby being brought into a world like this; I cried for myself. The news about Myla – how she'd known my secret, and how she'd been willing to hurt me if it meant I'd stay with her – confirmed all my fears about her. It felt like I no longer had a sister: I could never go back to live in Galex again.

Nobody got much sleep for the rest of the night. Anxieties were high in case there were more Saurians close by. We felt suddenly unprepared and exposed. The mood was sombre, after the deaths of two of our own.

"You couldn't have known," Brown spoke gently, voicing another fear I was harbouring: that I was responsible for the attack. My negligence as a leader had left two dead.

"I should have had us all on standby. Should have known the dangers. How did they get past the guards? We had the camp covered."

A clamour from the wooded area behind us brought the answer. Two recruits came flying back into the clearing.

"It's Rhea. She's been killed," one panted, delivering the news. "I think it must have taken both Saurians – she's a mess. Beheaded."

My head fell into my hands, grief overtaking all else. It

took several minutes before I felt composed enough to look up.

"This is what we're facing. You can't think of Saurians as mindless beasts anymore. They're getting smarter, working together to attack. It means our mission is more important than ever."

*

When dawn broke around four, we set about burying our dead. The recruits all pitched in to dig the holes, collect flowers and find stones to mark the graves. We gave them a short ceremony as we laid them to rest.

We felt there wasn't much choice but to keep moving. We'd seen the creatures becoming more organised – they'd ambushed us and cost us lives. We couldn't risk a larger nest working against us like that, not when the result could be catastrophic. This time we'd be ready, though – we wouldn't make the same mistake again.

*

Sleep eluded me as we all tried to nap in the afternoon, aware we'd be doing shifts awake overnight when the Saurians were at their strongest. We'd set up the camps early ready for the morning, the hope being we'd launch our attack at their weakest time.

As yet, the Ys seemed to be showing no ill effects from yesterday's vaccine injection. I could only hope Ilana's plan would work and allow me to not only reverse the effects on the Ys, but still give us the chance to weaken the nest. With a lump of guilt settled in my stomach since Tyra's death, I needed to give my recruits a better survival chance when facing our foes.

I had to talk to Brown. It wasn't going to be an easy conversation. How do you tell the person you love that you were prepared to risk the lives of Ys to give Xs a better chance? He'll understand, my brain said rationally. He knows you have to put the baby first. His heart would say different though, I knew. I could only hope it didn't damage our relationship beyond repair.

Even with Ilana's plan, we had injected the Ys with a potentially deadly poison. We could have given them all a placebo or just ditched Myla's plan altogether once we'd left the city. Although I doubted Tyra was the only recruit she had watching me. If she'd warned her spies to expect injections, their absence would have been a clear indication that we had rejected her plan. Now I knew she wanted Brown dead, no matter what. And she knew about the baby. I also knew she'd stop at nothing to get me back to Galex. I had to have my wits about me – her gaining Tyra's trust had taught me that she had a longer reach than I'd anticipated.

At least we were far enough away from the city to put Ilana's plan into action without Myla being alerted to it. Even if she had more spies, we were several days' travel out of the city – she was too far away to have much immediate influence. For now, my priority had to be getting Brown and then the rest of the Ys onside and preparing the recruits for battle.

Myla would have to wait.

*

"Can we talk?" I pulled Brown to one side, less bothered by the glances I was getting from the recruits who were also avoiding sleep. I knew they'd all be gossiping, yet it no longer seemed that important. After facing the Saurians as a group, I could see a chance to unite us all. I just had to get Brown on board.

We walked out of camp, but not far, still wary after yesterday's ambush. We found a small clearing, and leant against a large sycamore, silent for several minutes, enjoying the sounds of nature. For a few minutes, we could have been anywhere, doing anything. I hoped this would be how it felt when we were finally free.

"So," Brown said finally, reaching for my hand. "What do you need to talk about?"

I took a deep breath. Here goes nothing. "The plan of attack." I paused. "The injections."

"I wondered if this was what it was about," he said smiling. This confused me – would you smile if you'd worked out you and all your friends had been poisoned? And your girlfriend was in on it?

"What do you know?" I asked carefully, searching his eyes for answers.

"Well, I'm only guessing, but it seemed strange to only inject the Ys. If it were just to kill us, I couldn't work out why we'd need to be brought on the mission. So, therefore, it must be a cure? For the mutations!" He finished, clearly proud of himself for his logical thought process. "It would be just like you to keep it secret from me: you wouldn't want to get my hopes up, in case it didn't work!" He beamed at me.

My heart sank. If only his theory was the truth. I realised I had to just come clean and be completely honest.

"Not quite. It is a vaccine, but before you get excited, there's a serious flaw. Untreated, the vaccine injected will kill you. It takes a few days for that to happen, but it will. Myla's idea was that if we sent you out as prey ahead of the real battle, the Saurians would feed on your infected blood and be weakened or killed themselves."

I looked at him sideways, to see how he was taking this. He looked crestfallen. I hurried on. "But Ilana and I have a very different plan. One that won't sacrifice the Ys but will help in the fight against the Saurians. I couldn't tell you before, as I needed you out here, and I couldn't risk raising anyone's, namely Myla's, suspicions."

"Okay," Brown answered, speaking slowly. "So, there's no risk to us then? Did you replace the vaccine with something harmless?" he asked quietly, eyes on the floor.

Here came the tricky part. "For you, yes. Ilana devised a placebo made up from saline. I couldn't in good conscience risk your life, not when we're having a baby. But with the rest of the Ys, that wasn't an option. We can cure them all though, and we will. You see, I had to think about the recruits' safety as well. If there's any way to help them in the attack –"

"So you used the vaccine," he cut me off, eyes boring into mine. "Was it a case of hoping just a few of them got sick early on so there'd be something to feed the Saurians? Kill a few of us off to even up the odds in a fight? They could all drop dead at any moment!" His eyes became wild as he realised the full implications of what I'd done. "You've put the safety of Xs above Ys! You're no different from your sister!"

"That's not fair!" I shouted, hurt by the comparison. "When you hear the full story, you'll understand why I had to take the chance, for all our sakes," I tried desperately to explain. "Plus, Ilana had worked out all the timings so we could reverse the effects before anyone died."

I wanted him to see it wasn't about Ys or Xs, but about taking a calculated risk to save the most lives.

The accusation in his eyes make me uncomfortable, though. Had I found it easier to play God with the lives of the Ys? Was I more like Myla than I wanted to admit? Another lump of guilt joined the one already sitting in my stomach.

"I get that there's danger for us all," Brown acknowledged after an awkward silence, hurt still radiating from his blue eyes. "But once again, the Ys are expendable. You knew what you were doing could be deadly, and that's why you made sure I was safe."

I hung my head, realising he was right.

"You were the one X I'd expected better from. I guess I was wrong."

And with that, he turned his back on me and walked away.

BROWN

SIXTEEN

I couldn't believe what she was telling me to begin with. Risking the lives of my friends without telling me? Keeping me safe, but knowingly endangering the rest of the Ys? I had to get away, so for the first time ever, I deliberately walked away from her.

If we'd been a normal boyfriend and girlfriend in a normal world, I could have walked off and taken as much space as I needed. As it was, in an unknown landscape potentially crawling with dangerous lizard hybrids, I had no real choice but to head back to camp. I was angry, but not hot-headed enough to venture further away and risk becoming a Saurian snack.

Plus, on the other hand, I had a secret too which I knew would hurt Cara. I'd kept the plot to assassinate Myla to myself to protect Cara. I still couldn't risk telling her – not yet. Not if it gave her a chance to try and save her sister, or distracted her from the attack and left her vulnerable to danger that way. I guessed we were both putting the baby first, even before each other. That was what being a parent was, I realised.

Despite what she'd done, keeping Cara and our child safe was still my priority.

The reflection on my own secret and the short walk into camp left me feeling calmer. Logically, I knew Cara had taken an educated risk – she was a planner and a commander. She was looking at the long game. She wasn't putting the Ys in any more danger than she would put her own recruits in, and if her strategy worked, she had actually saved us from the fate designed by Myla. I owed it to her to at least listen to the plan she and Ilana had cooked up and trust that they had only done what was necessary for the benefit of us all.

I didn't have long to wait. Cara arrived back at the camp shortly after I did, looking fairly sheepish. Her eyes scanned around, looking for me. When she spotted me, she nodded, before pulling Ilana aside.

Their conversation looked intense and fairly urgent. When Cara put her fingers in her mouth to whistle loudly and draw everyone's attention, I realised she was ready to announce their plan and confess to the Ys what they'd done. The grim look on her face told me she wasn't relishing the prospect. I resolved to back her up – they might need a Y voice on their side when they came clean about the vaccine. I had to trust in the choice Cara had made and in her feelings for me and the baby.

"Everyone gather together," she called once she'd got the camp's attention. "There's a few things we need to talk about before tomorrow's attack."

The recruits quickly settled themselves around the

fire, with the Ys hanging back, clearly unsure if the tactical discussion involved them as well.

"You too," Cara added, addressing the lurking Ys directly.

Cautiously, they sank to the ground, perching uncomfortably on the group's perimeter.

"We all know what we'll be facing tomorrow," she began, the only betrayal of her nerves being her tightly clasped hands. "But I'm still not sure if you've all grasped the enormity of the task ahead of us."

The recruits murmured uneasily, looking from Cara to each other.

"But we've trained for this. We're ready," one with long dark hair piped up.

"Don't get me wrong, I'm not putting you down," Cara continued, keen to strike the right note.

"However, last night we faced an attack from two Saurians and we all witnessed the devastation they cause. We can't be complacent – a large nest is a formidable prospect and I'd be failing you if I didn't make it clear just how big the threat to our lives will be." Cara's eyes met mine.

"It's very likely that many of us will die in the fight. So, if there was any way I could give us better odds, or improve our chances, I'd grab it tight with both hands."

"What are you saying?" Becka asked slowly, a frown creasing her forehead.

I shifted my feet so I was kneeling. There was a tension in the air; it felt like we were all waiting for a revelation.

"I'm saying, that there was one option. To try and weaken at least some of the nest before we attacked."

Audible sounds bubbled up as this news was digested. Cara held up a hand, signalling for silence.

"It's not straightforward though and nothing's guaranteed. I'll let Ilana explain the science but," her eyes scanned the Ys, "ultimately know that the decision was mine."

I kept my eyes trained on Cara, refusing to look at my friends until Ilana had spoken.

"Progress has been ongoing with our vaccination programme," she began, a flush rising up her neck, visible under her dark roots.

"We've developed what we think is an antidote to the mutant gene which leads to the transformations in Ys." Now it was the Ys turn to burst into mutterings, peppered with exclamations and gasps as this information was processed.

Striker, a large hunter sitting next to me, gripped my wrist hard.

"Wait," he interrupted, drawing Ilana's attention. "Are you saying what I think you're saying?"

"If you think I'm saying we've found a cure for the Epidemic, then no I'm not."

"Sorry," she added quickly, seeing the widespread dismay and deflation that followed. "That is still our ultimate aim."

"What our discovery does, is it reacts with the chromosome that mutates with the virus – namely the Y chromosome, and destroys it. Meaning, it kills it. And its host."

"Hang on, let me get this straight," Striker continued, crossing his bulky arms across his front. "This antidote kills the bit that will react with the virus but also kills the person?"

Ilana nodded. "That's exactly it. We're hoping that in the future we can build on our work –"

"So why are you telling us now?" Striker stood up and stepped forward, looking as if he was squaring up for a fight, his hazel eyes suspicious. "I don't suppose it would have anything to do with those needles you jabbed in our arms the other day, would it?"

A rumble arose from the Ys, as they digested this accusation.

Cara jumped in. "It was, but that's not the end of the story. Our plan was never to let you die."

"You'd better start explaining pretty fast, then," Striker threatened. I stood up and placed a hand on his chest. "Because at the minute it seems like we've not got a lot to lose."

"Give her chance to talk," I urged him quietly. I couldn't read the look he gave me.

Cara continued. "I don't blame you for being angry. In your shoes, I would be too. But we had to make a decision that would hopefully benefit the most people."

"Xs you mean," a Y shouted.

"No, people," Cara repeated firmly. "We know how to reverse the effect of the vaccine you've been injected with. We always planned to administer a cure."

"So why go to all the trouble of injecting us in the first place?" Striker asked incredulously, arms still firmly crossed.

"Because," Ilana picked up, "the vaccine reacts with the blood of a Y to create a deadly cocktail – deadly to Ys, but also, I suspect, deadly to Saurians."

The penny dropped. If they were going to weaken the Saurians, they had to inject us – the vaccine on its own was useless: it needed Y blood to become fatal.

"So, what's your plan, feed us to them? Get them to eat us in the hope we'll poison them? This definitely sounds like it's been cooked up by your sister!" Striker practically growled at Cara, so angry was he. I could see uncertainty in his eyes too though – were the Ys expendable? Would we be sacrificed for the greater good?

"It might have been Myla's plan, but we have a better idea which will mean we are all alive to face the hopefully weakened Saurians tomorrow." She looked back at Ilana and nodded.

"We need samples of your blood – the more we have, the better our chances with this. If each Y here would donate, say, a pint of blood, I think we will have enough to have a real chance at harming the Saurians ahead of the fight."

"And I'm guessing you can reverse the effects on us once we've donated?" I asked.

"We came prepared." Ilana rummaged in her medical cool box and held up vials.

"Antibodies, extracted from X blood plasma. I made sure we had more than enough for all of you."

"Now let's just be clear," Striker was starting to look a bit less aggrieved. "You take our blood. We take yours. We go back to normal?"

"That's a fairly simplistic overview of the science, but essentially yes," Ilana agreed. "The vaccine we've already given you has flooded your blood with antigens that you can't fight off. For whatever reason, it's only Xs who are protected from this virus. So, I isolated the antibodies that occur in our blood to protect us, and now we'll inject them into your bloodstream."

"Meaning we'll be able to fight the virus too?"

"That's right."

I looked at Cara. She was still nervous, stood with hands clasped behind her back. I smiled faintly at her, making sure I caught her eye. She smiled back. I understood why she'd acted the way she had now. As a commander and protector, she had made a difficult decision. It still didn't sit easily with me, the risk she'd taken with Y lives, but logically it was the best solution. It reminded me that she was a natural leader: one who was prepared to make awful choices, and who sometimes had to rely on the roll of a dice to secure a better outcome.

"How are you planning on using our infected blood against the Saurians?" 6 asked, as the remaining Ys began to look more at ease with the plan.

"We could do with as many dead animals as we can get our hands on. Hunters, you'll be best placed to help us with this, but it'll need to be a group effort. We'll inject your infected blood into their corpses, leave them surrounding the nest –"

"Like a fairy circle of death," Becka joked.

"And hope with everything we've got that they take the bait." Ilana looked thoughtful. "They should," she added. "They might be evolving fast, but they're still beasts at heart, driven by the need for survival."

"You'll still have lots of questions," Cara picked up, "and we'll answer as best we can. But time is of the essence. We think you should be safe from any negative effects for another 12 hours, but the sooner we reverse the vaccine, the sooner we can all relax. Until we have to face a bunch of killer lizards," she deadpanned.

"For now, can all recruits start hunting – stick in groups of three, and don't stray any closer to the nest – retrace our steps if you need to."

"And Ys," Ilana instructed, pulling more medical equipment out of her bag, "I need your blood, and then you need this." She held high a handful of vials: the antibodies which would save our lives.

"Just before I let you shove anything else into my arm," Striker towered over Cara and Ilana, "tell me why you're bothering with all this. Why not just do what your sister suggested, and let us die?"

Cara squared her jaw and looked up at him. "Because we are not all like her. Because this is the right thing to do. I don't want to live in a world where I can help some people live by letting others die, regardless of whether they are X, Y or Z. I wouldn't want anyone growing up in a world like that." At this last point, she looked meaningfully at me and I knew she was thinking about the baby.

"Plus, on a practical level, you could be helpful in the fight. The more warriors we have, the better our survival rates. If you stay and help us, you'll be free to leave after, to make your own way. I can totally understand why you might not want to return to Galex, and I promise you, no one will stop you if you decide to go."

Seemingly mollified, Striker sat on the log next to Ilana's makeshift doctor's lab. He stuck his arm out.

"Fine. Do what you've got to do."

MYLA

SEVENTEEN

I'd been very careful to hide my feelings as Cara and her gang left for the mission. I refused to get all misty eyed as my sister went off, knowing full well she was planning to abandon me. A part of me even toyed with the idea of just letting her go. But I couldn't. I'd done so much for her; worked hard to keep her safe for years. Since Dad. I had a feeling that without her, I'd give in to the darkness completely. It was threatening to consume me now, with the bond between us stretched to breaking point. I was like a child holding onto a balloon for dear life: I felt that same dread at losing something precious, something you will never get back. In my case, I would lose part of myself.

A knock at the door. Delilah entered, one of a handful of recruits who'd stayed behind in the city. I still needed enough muscle to keep things in order and although unlikely, a Saurian attack was always a possibility. It goes without saying I kept behind the ones who were most easily influenced.

"Did you find one?"

"I did," she answered, smiling a toothy grin. Her frizzy mane stood on end, making her resemble a bedraggled lion.

Turning briefly, she pulled forward a Y – a runner, as requested.

"Number?" I barked.

"5," he responded sullenly, clearly on edge about the reason he'd been summoned.

"Delilah, can you fetch Mags for me, please? She'll know what it's about," I asked sweetly. She nodded and practically skipped off, her wiry frame giving her a loping walk. I had no doubt that she was enjoying the trust I was placing in her.

I looked at the Y in front of me. Small, Asian. I caught sight of the pulse in his neck, a reminder that the blood running in his veins was different from that of mine. It told me he was afraid, and well he should be.

"Congratulations," I said, causing him to jump and briefly make eye contact.

"For?" he asked cautiously, clearly thinking that if I was pleased, it probably didn't bode well for him.

"You are going to have a key role in preserving the future of Galex. If you do well, you'll save countless Y lives and you'll bring my sister home to me." The wary expression in his dim eyes suggested he had no clue what I was talking about.

Mags and Delilah entered before I could share anything else. Mags carried a needle, tapping the end to check the mechanism would smoothly deliver its contents into the correct bloodstream.

"Here we are," I announced, enjoyed the theatre. "Your way to become a hero!"

The Y looked with horror at the needle. "Wh-what's going on?" he stammered, backing up into the corner of my office. Delilah had already sidled behind him though, and she caught his arms tight and pressed him down into the chair opposite my desk.

"We've found a way to stop you from turning into a Saurian!" I shared, smiling in what I thought was a benevolent way.

He looked confused. Distrust, hope and fear all fought for dominance in his face.

"For real?"

"Sort of." Mags expertly plunged the needle into the top of his spindly arm.

"An unfortunate side effect is your death." I chuckled, noting that fear had won the fight.

"Why are you doing this?" he screeched, jumping up and backing into the corner again, like a trapped animal.

"Because I need to get my sister back. You have about 48 hours before the effects of the vaccine will kill you. If you run at a steady pace, you should find Cara and the rest of them at their camp." I thrust a bit of paper at him.

"Here – the co-ordinates for the large nest they were attacking first. They should be somewhere nearby, and if you're lucky, some of them will still be alive."

"I'm doing nothing for you! After what you've just done to me, you're insane if you think I'm gonna help you!" the Y snarled, hatred having overpowered fear now.

I sighed. "Then do it for yourself. If you find them within

217

the 48 hours and tell them you've been injected, they have the means to reverse the vaccine and keep you alive. Which means there's no point you wasting time here with us – get going." I made a shooing motion with my hands.

Still breathing heavily, unsure if this was all part of an elaborate trap, he started edging towards the door, clearly itching to at least get out of my sight.

"Just be sure to pass on a message to my sister. In another 48 hours, I'm going to inject the rest of the Ys with the same vaccine. They will die. Unless, of course, someone gives them the antibodies to reverse it."

I grabbed the Y's face and looked him square in his eyes.

"And the only way that will happen is if I see her back in Galex, with or without that pathetic excuse of a Y she apparently trusts more than her own flesh and blood."

Understanding finally dawned in his eyes.

"And if she refuses?"

"She won't. All you have to do is give her the message. If she comes back, the Ys will be saved. If she doesn't, they die. The only thing you have to worry about is finding them before you –" and I made a cutting motion across my neck.

The Y realised he had no real choice. With a deep breath, he shot out of my office on a mission to save not only himself, but every other Y in Galex.

CARA

EIGHTEEN

Several hours after being told about the vaccine and our plan, all Ys had donated blood and been given the antibody treatment. A whole host of animals had also been collected: rabbits, birds, even a badger.

"In case the Saurians are picky eaters," Callie quipped.

Ilana had painstakingly injected infected blood into each one. Before night fell, they had been planted along the outside edge of the nest, as close as anyone dared to get. All we could do now was wait – if it worked, the battle would still be tough, but we might have a chance of getting through it.

"So, assuming they have a delicious feast of vaccinated blood tonight, how long do you predict it'll take before the effects start to be felt?" I asked Ilana, trusting to her judgement.

"With the Ys it takes several days, but I think it'll be less with a Saurian. Because their genetic code is already mutated, I think the antigens will attack swiftly. I'd hope they'd be significantly weakened in about 12 hours."

"So, the attack can still go ahead tomorrow?"

She nodded. "You might want to push it back a few hours to midday, but I wouldn't want to give them longer in case the effects are only limited. You wouldn't want them back at full strength."

"Definitely not. Midday it is then. Until then, we wait."

A cloud of uncertainty settled on me. With all our lives hanging in the balance, it would be a long 12 hours.

*

The evening passed slowly. All I could think about was Brown. Had he forgiven me? He'd seemed more understanding, once the plan had been fully explained, but it still felt like there was a distance between us. The accusation that I was more like Myla than he'd thought had stung me. A tiny voice inside me kept questioning if he was right.

Would I have endangered the lives of the recruits in the same way? Some soul searching told me no, I wouldn't. The rational part of my brain reminded me that they were highly trained and the best weapon we had against the Saurians – it might have been different if all our roles were reversed and we were relying on the Ys to lead the attack. Another voice told me society was to blame – I'd grown up being told that Ys were dangerous and needed to be kept at arm's length. I feared this mindset had affected me more than I'd realised.

I could only resolve to do better in the future. Never to treat Ys as less important again. Never to treat Brown as less important. Assuming we made it through tomorrow alive, of course.

*

The night dragged by too. I'd learned the hard way about guarding the camp tightly, meaning nothing was left to chance. I slept on and off for a few hours, but my dreams were so vivid, I kept waking with a start. One minute a Saurian was attacking me, the next I was a Saurian attacking Brown. I'd wake up panting, covered in a sheen of sweat, the tiny being inside me drumming a tattoo on my insides. I was almost glad when morning finally dawned, and I could face real monsters rather than my own inner demons.

There was a surprisingly calm atmosphere building up to the final stage of our mission. In half an hour, we'd be face-to-face with the biggest Saurian nest that any of us had ever seen. We could only hope that our plan had worked and at least some of them were already incapacitated. Despite our weaponry and the skill of the recruits, without that I wouldn't be betting on our chances. Not after what we'd seen the other night.

The morning began with a blood-red sunrise, misting the landscape with a pearlescent pink glow. Despite the beauty of a rose-tinged dawn, I could only hope this wasn't a warning about the bloodshed to follow.

The camp was fairly muted throughout breakfast, and light training took up the rest of the morning. I didn't want the recruits to tire themselves out, but realised the better prepared they felt, the better chance they'd have. At least going through the motions reminded them that they could do what they'd been trained to in their sleep, so ingrained was it in their muscle memory.

As midday approached, the atmosphere was highly charged. Some of the Ys still seemed resentful of the vaccination plan, and I got used to the sideways, suspicious glances. Brown was quiet. Head down for most of the morning, I barely got the chance to get near him, let alone speak to him. I'd need to before we left, in case it was the last chance I'd ever get. We couldn't go into this with our fight not having been fully resolved.

I needed him to know I understood his anger, his sadness. I was determined to prove to him that I could still be the person he thought I was.

*

I'd decided to leave our camp where it was. With any luck, most of us would be back here later on.

Just before the agreed departure time, everyone seemed to be milling around, slightly at a loss.

"Ok everyone," I began, aware of how important these final words would be. "I'll keep this short. We know what we have to do. We just don't know how hard it's going to be. Even if the Saurians have taken the bait we left, there's no way of knowing how weakened they'll be, if at all."

"We might be lucky, and they're all dead already!" a recruit called out.

"That would be great, but I think we should be prepared for the worst. We could well be walking into a large nest at full strength. It will be more dangerous than anything you've ever faced. Two were a challenge: we all saw that these beasts are changing. They're smarter, they're beginning to work

BROWN

together. This will make our job harder, but at the same time it makes a victory over them even more vital. We can't leave them to continue to evolve – where would that end? A world run by Saurians, where humans are hunted down like rats? Our only option is to act swiftly and act now.

"Remember what I've taught you. Be alert, be instinctive. Trust your gut. Your body will warn you of the danger before you see it – never ignore a feeling.

"Be prepared. Double check your weaponry now. Play to your strengths. We've practised scenarios again and again and again – we are ready. Stay focused and look out for each other. And remember – whatever happens, you are all protecting our future and the future of every other survivor."

Coming alive at my words, the recruits hugged and high-fived each other, boosted by adrenaline now the moment was finally here. My pride at their bravery almost burst from my chest: I closed my eyes momentarily, willing a future into existence where all of these young girls came back alive.

*

The formation of the attack was simple: Xs up front, in an arrow shape. The fastest were going to infiltrate the nest first, get an idea of what had happened, and throw in some grenades that had been found in an old army surplus store. I wasn't confident they'd be powerful enough to destroy a Saurian, but they should add to the confusion and hopefully disorientate them. The recruits would then attack in waves, five at a time, with each wave targeting a Saurian in the hopes of bringing them down.

With any luck, the infected blood would have taken its toll on their immune systems, making them easier to overcome.

The Ys were the next line of defence. I'd paired them in runner/hunter duos, the idea being that four of them together could tackle any beasts that got through. With a lesser degree of training, my hope was that they wouldn't even be needed.

"You okay?" Ilana caught up with me as we made our way cautiously to the nest.

"I will be, once I've spoken to Brown. We can't go ahead with this while we're arguing. It wouldn't be right."

She turned her liquid eyes on mine. "You had limited choices, and he will see that. You have a responsibility for so many people – and top of that list has to be your child. You acted as a mother, first and foremost. Make him see that."

She hugged me fiercely, before taking off to lead the assault from the front, only turning briefly to add, "And make sure you keep yourself safe."

*

Turns out, Brown must have been thinking about it as much as I had.

I knew that to avoid the worst of the assault, I'd need to assume a role from the back – let the recruits attack hard, and then provide them with back up. With this aim, I could legitimately fall back, and keep just ahead of the Ys as we made our approach.

As I hung back, Brown caught me up and fell in step

beside me. Already nervous about what we were a[
face, I exhaled deeply before turning to face him.

His hand brushed mine.

"I'm sorry," I started. "I know I risked the lives
friends, and I probably wouldn't have been so cava
was with Xs. All I can do is strive to be better. I wa
better. For you."

"I know," he responded quietly. "You did w
thought was right. I can't honestly say that if I'd be€
same situation, I'd have acted any differently."

"Really?" I asked, a lightness overtaking m‹
understanding raised my hopes that things could g‹
the way they usually were between us.

"We come from a really messed up world. X‹
– everything is so complicated." He took my han
despite the fact we were surrounded by people.

"But we can make a better world. For us. An‹
one." He placed a hand softly on my stomach.

"Just keep safe. I need you. I need the futι
planned."

Just as Ilana had done, he hugged me tightly.

"I need you too," I answered, breathing in
Creating a memory, just in case I wasn't able to
more.

"See you on the other side." He kissed me br
fell back.

We had arrived at the outskirts of the nest.

NINETEEN

As we got closer to the target, we all got quieter as the nerves really started to kick in. The Ys fell back, covering the exits from the wooded area which contained the nest. All seemed still and calm from out here: we could only hope that was because the Saurians were dead or nearly so, and not just napping after a busy night. In the morning light, the recruits suddenly looked very young and very scared – for perhaps the first time, we all understood what we were walking into.

Striker and I were paired together. He glanced slyly at me.

"So, you and the Commander, hey?" he whistled slowly, shaking his head, eyes wide in disbelief.

"She's … special," I replied, keen not to get drawn into anything which could distract me at this point. I kept one eye on Cara, watching her settle about 15 feet ahead of us, clambering a few branches up a sycamore tree. She wedged herself in, silently directing the recruits leading the assault with her gestures.

"Hey man," he replied, arms up in a conciliatory gesture, "your business."

We were directed to a partially hidden corner on the outskirts of the woods and took cover behind a huddle of bushes. We'd been given weapons, which came as a surprise to most of the Ys. I could see them looking at Cara differently as she doled them out, could see them thinking she perhaps wasn't so bad, at least not like her sister. Luckily for me, Striker was great with a bow and arrow so that was reassuring at least. I was given a sort of machete, which looked pretty mean too.

"If we hide really well, we could just sit the whole thing out and then make a run for it," Striker joked. His smile didn't reach his eyes though, so I knew he was afraid. I chuckled along, trying to help him lighten the mood. My stomach was in knots. Part of me did want to run and get as far away as possible. I knew I'd never be able to look Cara in the eyes again if I did that, though. I had to be brave, for her and the baby. With her stationed only metres ahead of us, I resolved not to let her out of my sight. For now, all we could do was settle in and wait.

I just prayed we both got through the next few days alive.

*

In the end, it all happened so quickly, running away was never a realistic option. One minute we were practically dozing, as the morning sun climbed in strength, the next an explosion of sound. Four mutants staggered out from the trees, pursued by various numbers of recruits. It was a bit like watching a well-choreographed dance being performed in front of me. The nerves had clearly disappeared in the heat of the battle and the recruits were magnificent to watch. The largest Saurian seemed unwell: it staggered, shaking, and fell to its knees pretty much as soon as it emerged. Blue blood was dripping from its fangs and it let out a guttural groan. Two recruits were swift to dispatch it once it had collapsed, swiping its throat from left to right. It knelt for a moment, stunned, before crashing to the ground. The second was also fairly easy to kill. It looked a bit worse for wear too, although not as bad as the first. I guessed the poison had been effective, just to different levels in the different beasts.

This one seemed more disorientated than anything else. Again, the recruits were masterful. Three rounded on it, one running back and forth, moving nimbly to avoid its swiping claws. Whilst it was distracted, another attacked from behind, incapacitating it by slashing its ankles. As it turned, shrieking, a third threw an axe with such precision, it struck directly between the eyes. Just to make sure, a final stab to the gut was administered, leaving no doubt it was definitely defeated.

The third mutant was trickier. It was smaller but definitely livelier; it seemed unaffected by any form of virus. We stayed hidden, watching it attack another pair of recruits, one of whom I recognised as Callie. They were doing their best to avoid its ferocious blows, whilst trying to get in some shots themselves. It looked like they were pretending though – every time they stabbed or shot an arrow, the Saurian plucked the weapon from its skin and tossed it away, as if it were nothing. I could see the pair begin to tire. Cara looked to be itching to intervene, but common sense kept her in the tree, her javelin trained on the Saurian as she tried to get a clear shot.

"Do we get involved?" I whispered to Striker.

"Not yet," he replied. "We're the last resort, remember? Let's see how the next few minutes play out."

We waited. The recruits kept trying. One went behind, one in front. The beast just swatted one with its tail and swiped dangerously close to the other. Shots were fired. Some hit their target, but it was like watching a child anger a wasp – it only seemed to make the situation worse. Cara's spear flew from her hand, skimming the beast's cheek but causing little physical damage. Responding with rage at her attempted attack, the Saurian slashed the younger recruit across her thigh. Blood poured, a velvety red, as she hit the ground. Teeth bared, claws ready, it pounced.

Thwack! An arrow flew from beside me.

"Bullseye!" shouted Striker, as we watched it strike the creature directly in the left eye. Time slowed, the beast swayed, seemingly paused in that moment. The remaining eye clouded, like milk spreading into a hot drink. With a wobble, it tumbled, crashing down with such force that the earth rumbled and shook. It didn't move again.

"Nice shot!" Cara called, clearly impressed and relieved by Striker's accuracy.

"Better luck next time, Commander!" he responded, a cheeky grin accompanying the pride on his face. Cara saluted him in return.

"Thanks," said the injured recruit weakly, ripping off part of her top to bandage her leg.

This last act turned out to be pointless though. The remaining Saurian had thrown off the recruits battling it, leaving them dazed. It sprang at the wounded recruit, jaws open. We could only watch in horror. Seconds later, mouth ringed red with blood, it turned in our direction.

"Bugger!" Striker breathed, as we realised his crack shot had given away our location. "Looks like we're next on its menu."

With Callic distracted helping another recruit who'd taken a beating, the beast circled our location.

From the corner of my eye, I could see Cara disembarking from her tree hideaway. All I could do was mentally will her to stay back and let us handle this.

"Can you do that arrow in the eye thing again?" I murmured, heart pounding.

"I can try." He took aim. Thwack!

This time the arrow went wide. The Saurian snarled, as if disgusted by this poor attempt on its life.

"Please don't tell me that was your last one," I said nervously.

"Okay I won't. But it was."

Suddenly the creature lunged. With one jump from its powerful legs, it was next to us, practically on us. I swiped wildly with my machete, dodging left and right as the beast swept its arms forward, trying to get a strike with those diamond-strength claws. Striker was also darting around, holding an axe. Every time the Saurian faced him, I'd jab with my knife, and vice versa when it faced me, he'd attack with the axe. Despite this elaborate dance, we seemed to be making extraordinarily little impact. All the while, those sharp talons were getting dangerously close. Finally, Striker seemed to decide enough was enough. With a yell, he launched himself at the beast's foot, ramming the axe down. It roared; he scrambled back. With alarming ease, it lifted its foot, axe and all, and advanced menacingly.

Swoosh! The Saurian stopped, seemingly pausing for thought. In slow motion, it crashed forward, leaving us to scramble back to avoid it crushing us as it fell like a dead weight. Sticking out from the back of its head was Cara's spear.

Striker and I stood agog, mouths open, staring at her. She bowed low.

"You're welcome. Thanks for the luck," she winked at Striker. He chuckled, clapping her and bowing in return.

At that moment, a sound penetrated my mind. Thudding footsteps, battle cries, shots. The rest of the recruits descended on us, chasing down a final target. With whoops and hollers, they fell upon the last Saurian standing: a particularly large and evil-looking beast. Jabs, uppercuts, whips, juts. You name it, they did it. The most impressive sight was watching Becka do a running jump before climbing the Saurian's back and plunging a knife directly into its skull. This blow seemed to be the clincher as it flapped around, trying to throw her off, but lost its balance. Once down, it was finished.

Striker and I lay on the ground side by side, panting.

"Man, that was close," he eventually wheezed.

"You're telling me," I answered, bone-tired all of a sudden.

The nest defeated, we lay for a few minutes, seemingly in shock.

"Is that all of them?" Cara asked, as Ilana returned last from the direction of the nest, a little battered and bruised looking, but remarkably together bearing in mind the fighting that had gone on.

She nodded. "Yup. We were lucky. About two thirds were dead when we charged the nest, and half of the rest were on their last legs. We only had to kill about six of them at their full strength. Good job too – there'd have been a lot more casualties if it weren't for the effects of the vaccine."

"Hear that?" Cara shouted. "The Ys were our saviours today. Never forget that."

I sat up, wincing from the bruises already blooming under my shirt, where the Saurian had caught me.

"You guys saved us, too," I added.

"We all did amazingly," Cara agreed. "But now, head back to camp, rest up. We all deserve a good night's sleep."

I realised she'd be counting on the fact that we could get away early, before the others woke up. Despite my exhaustion, relief flooded me, making me feel more alive than ever. Our future was still intact – we'd made it through! After the competent display from the recruits, I knew Cara would feel confident leaving Ilana to lead them against the smaller nests, particularly as she'd preserved some infected blood. I stood up, ignoring my aching limbs for now.

"Come on, man," I called to Striker, whose eyes stayed firmly shut.

"Wake me up when it's time to fight the next lot."

*

It felt so good to finally collapse in a heap back at camp. Everything hurt, from my brain to the tips of my toes. I felt like even a week spent sleeping solidly wouldn't be enough to fully restore my weary bones.

Five minutes, though. That was what I got. Five minutes of rest. Eyes closed, mind drifting, body relaxing, before a shout.

"Look! Is that Brown 5? What the hell is he doing here?"

On hearing this, I sat bolt upright. It was 5, running determinedly for the camp, a grim expression on his face. I staggered up, needing to find out what had happened, because the look on his face told me that whatever it was, it wasn't good.

CARA

TWENTY

By the time the Y reached us, he was wheezing as he breathed in, and staggering rather than running. He must have been going full pelt for as long as his body would let him: he looked on the verge of collapse.

Brown was up and over to him as soon as he got close.

"Hey dude, what's the matter? You look terrible! What's going on, man?"

Despite everyone's exhaustion, a buzz of energy rippled through the camp. What had led to a Y tracking us down like this?

Brown refilled his canteen and passed it to the panting Y. He gulped the water down with the same determination that a snake swallows an egg. It took him several minutes to recover enough to even speak.

"She's injected me," he panted, eyes wide with despair. "With a vaccine that'll kill me. She said you can cure me?" He scanned the faces around him until his gaze settled on me. As if seeing me for the first time, he lunged at me, grabbing me around the waist as he sank to his knees. My heart quickened briefly, before I realised desperation, not anger, was driving this contact.

"Please!" he begged.

Brown released his arms from me gently, but firmly. "What do you mean? Who injected you?"

"The Boss!" He gasped, still struggling to breathe normally after his run. "I don't know how long I've got left."

"When were you injected?" Ilana asked, already rooting in her medical bag for her stash of antibodies.

"Yesterday morning. Early, like soon after sun's up. I think that's about …"

"36 hours, give or take." Ilana was business-like as she swiftly prepared a syringe. "You should be okay, but I wouldn't want to risk leaving this much longer. Arm," she demanded.

The Y held out his arm, eyes still afraid. Ilana smoothly pierced his skin and we watched the needle slide seamlessly in, releasing the antidote in a matter of seconds. When she'd finished, he flopped back, clearly drained.

"Is that it? Will I live?"

"For now," Ilana answered, placing her equipment away again.

"How about we sort you out some food and you tell us what's going on? Because this whole thing isn't making a lot of sense right now." Brown's eyes settled on mine – something was happening.

"I've a message. From your sister." As his eyes met mine, dread filled my body.

What was she planning?

*

"She said she was going to do *what*?"

The new Y was on his second wood-pigeon thigh when he managed to get out the details of what had happened.

"Inject the rest of the Ys," he smacked his lips, nibbling the last bit of flesh off the bone. "She said she'd wait 48 hours and then do it."

I sat down heavily. This was unlikely to just be an idle threat. Myla had already proven she saw Ys as less than human, as expendable. I didn't doubt she'd see them all drop down dead and feel no remorse.

"She said that if you go back, you can give them antibodies. Which I guess is what you just gave me?" He looked so tired and confused, Brown slung an arm around him.

"We did, buddy. You'll be fine in no time. And we'll get this sorted so the others are all okay, too."

"She was on about a Y too, one that her sister trusts more than her." Looking thoughtful, 5 turned his gaze on Brown and me, cogs clearly turning. "And I'm guessing that's you?" he said to Brown. "Did I miss something?"

"I think we all missed something," 6 piped up. "Seems there's been some funny business going on for a while." He looked pointedly at Brown.

"Looks like you have some explaining to do," Striker pitched in.

With the eyes of the camp on us, it was time to let everyone in on our secret. With Myla raising the stakes, I had no choice but to come clean and trust in my relationship with the recruits.

*

I spoke for what must have been about three minutes, but felt like a hundred. Silence reigned as I explained about the baby, Brown and me, our plan to leave. Everything was on the line. Total honesty. With Brown holding firm onto my hand, I knew he approved: if we were to get both the Xs and Ys onside, nothing else would do.

"But it turns out, Myla had already found out I was pregnant. She was using Tyra and God knows who else to spy on us. She also got wind of our escape plan. Which is why," I finished up, suddenly self-conscious after such a long period of quiet, "she's done this. She'll stop at nothing to get me back to Galex."

"Okay, I get that she hates Ys and doesn't care about killing us," 6 asked, once I'd finally stopped talking. "But how can she be sure you'd go back to save them? You could still take off and look after number one. Plus, why is she so desperate to have you in Galex? Seems to me she's not really a family kind of person. What makes you so special to her?"

Brown interrupted before I could answer. "You forget that Cara isn't like her sister," the authority in his voice adding a sense of calm. I could see clearly for the first time how he was trusted by his friends: they looked up to him, respected him.

"To do this, Myla was taking a gamble, yes. Cara could have ignored 5's message and still decided to escape. However, Myla knows her, as do I. She's kind and fair – she would be an exceptional leader. Myla knew that if she threatened the lives of others, Cara would respond, whether those lives belonged to Xs or Ys."

I could feel my face grow hot as Brown spoke about me so passionately. Despite my fears over Myla, my heart was full. I realised how lucky I was to have him in my corner. Whatever my sister had in store for me, his support gave me hope that together, we could withstand it.

"So, she'll go back?" Striker's face was anxious, and he was clearly itching to get going.

I nodded. "I have no choice. I thought we could get away, but the price is too high. This latest action by Myla is a clear red flag too – I can't leave her in charge of a community where she can threaten murder whenever she's challenged."

Striker nodded, appraising me. Again, he looked to Brown, clearly waiting for his seal of approval.

"As to why she wants me back so badly, I'm not sure I can answer that anymore. I know that for a long time, she thought her main role in life was protecting me. She has saved my life more than once. I wish I could say that was the only motive, though. My fear is I've become a kind of possession, something to control. When she found out about Brown and the baby, she realised she was losing power over me. She simply isn't prepared to let that go."

"Have you thought about what she might do to you, though?" Ilana interjected. "Or Brown? We already know she wants him dead." Her concerns mirrored my own.

"Don't worry about me," Brown butted in. "My only concern is seeing Cara and the baby safe. Saying that, we can't let her do this. We have to go back."

"I could go alone," I began, but before I'd finished Brown was shaking his head.

"No. We go together. No way are you facing this alone."

"He's right," spoke Callie. "But it's not just you two against her. It's all of us."

The recruits nodded, murmurs of support spreading around the group.

"It's you we're loyal to, not Myla. You know us, and you've helped us more than you know," Becka said.

Ilana chimed in too. "You may well need us. Myla is clever and ruthless. She won't give up without a fight. Plus, she'll have at least two more recruits on her side – Mimi and Chantelle haven't been seen since we arrived back at camp."

I shook my head. "More spies," I said bitterly.

"But the rest of us," Callie added, "are on your side. I think it's fantastic that you're going to be a mum. You'll be brilliant. You've certainly always been a maternal guide for us lot." The rest of the recruits agreed. My heart filled again: the thought of facing my sister seemed less daunting with so many supporting me.

"What about you guys – are you coming back with us?" Brown addressed the runners.

A few shook their heads, evidently not happy to go back to the Galex regime when it was clear they didn't have to. Striker, Browns 5 and 6 all stood by Brown though.

"We are. We can't let our friends down. We know how they feel – being a ticking time-bomb waiting for the vaccine to kill us." Striker shot me a look at this point.

"Plus, if the plot to get rid of the Boss went as planned, I wanna be there to see that."

"Plot?" I asked, picking up on his words, noticing from Brown's expression that something was being kept from me.

He turned towards me, pulling me aside after shooting Striker a look that said, you and your big mouth.

"Before we set off, there is something I need to confess."

MYLA

TWENTY-ONE

"Is it done?"

Orla stood in front of me, white coat gleaming. Her curls bobbed gently as she nodded.

"All Ys injected, as requested. Your idea worked – sleeping pills ground into their food, then a night-time vaccination."

"Excellent. Were any missed?"

"I think a couple, who'd obviously not ingested enough sedative. But don't worry, Delilah was on hand to deal with them."

I looked admiringly at Orla: she spoke without emotion about the deaths of Ys. It must be the scientist in her: she viewed them as guinea pigs, test subjects. This coldness was useful.

"And the other on-going project? You said you had more to share."

"We do." Orla smiled for the first time since entering my office. She withdrew a sealed tube from the wide pocket of her lab coat and several capped syringes, all filled with the same viscose substance. A hazy blue liquid swilled gently.

"Extracted from Saurian venom. I'm much more confident we've cracked it this time. We haven't tested it yet, but if we've got it right, it should transform a Y in minutes. How you control them will be down to you."

I told hold of one of the syringes, bringing it close to my face. "Imagine what we could do with this," I mused.

My thoughts were interrupted though. A commotion outside my door. Shouts echoed, a scream. Footsteps trampled down corridors, voices bellowed. Y voices.

Orla looked as startled as I felt. "What's going o –"

A gaggle of Ys burst in. A tall one, with sad, sunken eyes seemed to lead them. They were armed with laughably primitive weapons, but seeing as we were outnumbered, I judged we'd need to cooperate for now at least.

"We're taking Galex over!" the tall one yelled, spittle flying into my face. "You and your lot will be getting what you deserve, at last!" A madness in his eyes told me to act passively for the time being.

Another two grabbed my wrists and tied them behind my back. The same treatment was doled out to Orla, despite her protestations.

I could feel the cold press of the syringe against my ankle. It gave me some relief to know I'd had the foresight to hide it in my boot as soon as I'd heard the shouts.

"Chuck them in the old caretaker's closet for now, along with the other one. Put any more we find in the old drawing room at the front."

The Y's sad eyes turned on me once more.

"We're just rounding up your lackeys – they'll get the

same treatment as you. And this one," he jabbed Orla in the waist. "We think a public execution is the only thing good enough for you. How does tomorrow sound for your final day on earth?"

His triumphant smile made me chuckle. He thought he had me. The smile faded a little in the face of my laughter. It faltered, wavering.

"You might need to hold off for a little bit longer. Did anyone notice anything strange about their arms this morning? Did it feel like, oh I don't know, you'd been given an injection maybe?"

Doubt and recognition dawned on the Y faces around me. Expressions clouded as arms were examined, and puncture holes discovered.

I looked at Orla. "I suppose we'd better let them in on our little secret, hadn't we?"

BROWN

TWENTY-TWO

I could have killed Striker there and then. If we were heading back to Galex, I wouldn't have been able to keep the planned rebellion from Cara any longer, but I'd have chosen a better way to reveal the fact that I'd kept the potential assassination of her sister to myself.

The sharp look she gave me after Striker's revelation told me I was in for it.

We headed to a corner of the camp away from the rest of the group, leaving them to finalise preparations for us leaving.

"What the hell –" Cara started. "What was the plan, kill Myla and keep me in the dark?"

"What could I have done?" I said, exasperated, as her frown accused me of deceit. My emotions inside were threatening to erupt in a fight between guilt and frustration. I knew it had been wrong to keep the information from Cara. But on the other hand, telling her risked putting both her and the baby in danger. And for what? To save the X who went out of her way to make our lives a misery?

"There was no choice. We had to get away and I couldn't see you stay to protect her. Not when she's a monster!"

Cara stayed quiet, arms folded, glaring. I carried on, realising if I was going to justify my decision, now was the time.

"I put you and the baby first. And yes, I put me first. Before a leader who divides us. Who treats us like animals. Who would see us all dead before she'd let her baby sister go." I was surprised to feel tears in my eyes. I think it caught Cara off guard too, as her expression softened.

"I'm sorry I didn't tell you, I'm sorry for lying, at least by omission. But I'm not sorry that she might be dead and I'm not sorry that I care more about us," I gestured to the three of us, including the one in Cara's tummy, as best I could, "than I do about Myla. Even if she is your sister." Finally spent, I took a deep breath and slowly exhaled, waiting for my heartbeat to return to its normal pace.

"Wow," said Cara. "That was quite a speech. It might have been more effective if you hadn't just had a go at me for putting Ys at risk. You've treated Myla as expendable too."

I ran my hand across my head, the stubbly regrowth prickling my palm.

"I know. I'm not saying what I did was right, same as what you did wasn't right. But it was what had to be done."

Looking each other in the eye, we appraised the other's actions. It seemed we were both guilty of endangering others for our own sake. I realised we were bonded for life now, governed by the same thought process: our child would always come first, no matter the cost elsewhere.

"I hate to interrupt whatever this is," Striker approached cautiously, gesturing between us with his hands. "But time is running out for our friends. We need to get moving as soon as, if the Boss is going to lay eyes on you in time to give out the antidote."

"He's right," I said to Cara. "We need to get going now."

Her green eyes never left mine. "Agreed. I'm not fully okay with this yet, but this is not the time."

I nodded. We could talk more after. Work it out fully. For now, the lives of the Ys had to be our priority.

"If I can make a suggestion?" It felt weird offering up my ideas to a group like this.

Cara leant to pick up her pack, as the rest of the camp were in the final stages of clearing up and getting ready to leave.

"5 and 6, if you're happy with this, I suggest you guys and me get Cara back to the city as fast as we can. That means we run. We can take turns carrying her."

Cara groaned. "Oh great, so I'm like a backpack? What a dignified return!"

"How else do we get you back in time to guarantee the Ys are safe?"

She sighed, clearly running through the options in her head. Finding no workable alternative, she snapped, "Fine. But anyone drops me and there'll be trouble!"

"What do the rest of us do, then?" Becka asked, as she wrestled a sleeping bag into its tiny cover.

"Follow as quickly as you can. You should get there about eight hours after us, if you make good time."

"Can't we try and keep up with you guys?" Callie chipped in, biting the edge of her nail. "None of us knows what you're going to face when you get back. I feel like we should be there for you."

Cara hugged her tightly, clearly grateful for the fact she cared.

"But the runners are trained to cover long distances fast. We'll need their speed if we're going to make it back in time. All of us trying to stay together risks our journey being slower."

"I'm scared for you, though. I mean, if they'll hurt Myla, what's to stop them hurting you too?"

"I won't let them," I spoke up.

"But there's more of them than you," Becka pointed out logically.

"It's a risk we have to take," Cara answered, letting Callie out of the embrace. "They'll need us, at least to start with, if they're going to get the antidote."

Ilana nodded. "We've only got limited supplies left here, but there's plenty more in the lab's safe. Only Mags, Orla and I know the passcode, and I doubt those two'll be giving it up. You can use the code as a bargaining chip if things turn nasty. Exchange your life for their lives. It should buy you some time to get out of the city, at least."

"I don't think it'll come to that though," 6 added. "We can vouch for you being different. The Ys are angry about the way the Boss's treated them. This isn't an X versus Y thing. It's a Y versus Myla thing."

"It's all fairly irrelevant anyway," Cara said. "We have no choice but to go back. I can't let Myla make me responsible for mass murder. But I also can't leave her to face whatever the Ys have planned, no matter how much she might deserve it."

"Look, we don't know what we'll face," I spoke to the group as a whole, keen to let them know I'd do everything I could to keep Cara safe. "But us Ys, we do know our friends. We won't stand by and let them hurt anyone. Cara will decide what happens to her sister, not them. She'll be the one in charge. You trusted her to lead you into a massive lizard nest, so trust her now." Smiles and chuckles acknowledged what we'd already accomplished and made us all feel somewhat invincible.

Callie nodded. "Just stay safe. And don't worry, we'll be right behind you."

*

We gathered few possessions, needing to travel light. It was a long run, and carrying Cara was going to put extra pressure on the three of us.

"You sure we can stop them? They're so angry, especially that Eeyore dude." 5 kept his voice low.

"I hope so." I turned to face him. "It's what'll happen once they've had the antidote that I'm worried about."

"Promise me – you'll help us get out in a hurry if we need to, me and Cara. No matter what happens, you'll let us go."

"Course, man, I promise."

He meant it, I could tell. He was on our side.

I just wish things had stayed that way.

CARA

TWENTY-THREE

Never again do I want to be carried on the back of a running Y. Feeling about as useless as a lump of wood, the journey back was uncomfortable to say the least. Brown, 5 and 6 all took turns in lugging me on their backs, with one running ahead, then resting while the others caught up. We carried on this awkward arrangement for about seven hours, before a proper rest and food stop was planned.

As soon as they'd refuelled though, we were back on the road. For my part, I just had to cling on round their necks, and hope they didn't trip up and leave me face-planted in the mud. After a while, I couldn't help but start to nod off, the rhythmic pace and thud of feet lulling me to sleep. I was rudely awakened frequently and painfully by any jarring movement, though. Each time, I could feel my body aching more than the last.

It was a long night. The rain splattered us on occasion, but the clouds cleared around three, giving us the most beautiful sky. Swirls of grey misted the horizon, punctured by the glitter of stars dotting the darkness. I could feel the enormity of the world against my own life. I wanted to share this with my child one day.

Morning dawned drearily at around five. Thanks to the quick pace and lack of stops, we were only a couple of hours out of Galex. If Myla was true to her word, we should reach the city before the vaccinations were fatal for the Ys.

We made one last pit stop for more food and water. The Ys were exhausted. 6's eyes were bloodshot, with huge bags sagging underneath. 5 lay flat, arms stretched wide. Brown seemed to be surviving on adrenaline alone, but his face was gaunt and anxious.

"What if we're too late?" he worried.

All we could do was hope there was time left to save them.

*

Seeing the city walls emerge from the landscape added to my anxiety. It still felt like home, but I was scared about what I'd find within. Were the Ys still alive? Was Myla still alive? From out here, there was no indication at all.

"Well, at least the whole place is still standing!" joked 6, his attempt to lighten the mood met with tense silence. He slowed his running pace as we approached the shadow of the city wall. Finally, 6 placed me gently on the ground. My joints were stiff, leaving me limping as the blood began to fully circulate again.

The Ys flopped to the ground for a final five-minute

break. I was grateful for a brief rest too, circling my ankles and massaging my shoulders. A wriggling inside my stomach told me the baby had awoken now the rocking motion of the runners had stopped. I felt drained, despite not having done any actual running myself. I worried about Brown – the others had no need to come into the city yet – we'd agreed they'd follow us in after an hour or so, after checking all was clear. We had to hope they could be extra support if needed, but couldn't ask them to walk blindly into a lion's den. But Brown was insistent he accompany me inside the walls – no matter what Myla had in store for him.

"There's no way I'm letting you go in alone, not when we have no idea who's in charge now."

The scared part of me was relieved he was adamant about this: the rest of me could only hope his presence wasn't a mistake.

5 and 6 were clearly concerned too.

"You sure you don't want us there with you from the get go, man?" 5 looked ready to stand right back up, despite rubbing his feet in his hands.

"Nah, it's best if you wait here and then come in shortly. They might not be expecting you, so if things have gone badly, you might be our only hope."

Brown and I stood, our aching muscles complaining. We could put this off no longer.

"Just … look after each other in there. No matter if it's Xs or Ys in charge, stick together. Hang in there – the cavalry can't be that far behind." 6 slapped Brown hard on the back and awkwardly patted my shoulder. I smiled quietly, heartened by this show of affection. I didn't say that the recruits would still be a way off – if anything were to happen inside the city walls, it was unlikely they'd be arriving in time to help out.

With my stomach turning somersaults, I almost willed myself in there now, just so I could see what was happening.

Turning towards the city we headed off, hands clasped together as we walked to our fate.

*

Once inside the walls, the city of Galex was silent. An eerie hush seemed to have descended in our absence. Shadows grew from corners as the sun hurried across the sky, and a cool breeze tickled my loose hair. I shivered involuntarily.

All was fairly quiet. It was early, but I'd expected a few more signs of life. The only movement was a few pieces of litter drifting in the breeze: a plastic bag, some abandoned cardboard. I kept to the shadows, feeling uncertain of my surroundings.

"Where do we head, the school building?" Brown asked.

"I guess so. There's no sign of anyone out here."

We kept moving, aware of our surroundings. It was so quiet, it felt deserted.

Something wasn't right.

It was then that hands grabbed us from behind.

*

The Ys didn't hurt us. They took our weapons and then let us continue to make our way.

When we reached the school, sounds of voices began to carry over to us. We didn't rush in but made a cautious path to the centre of the grounds.

The scene in the courtyard was like something out of an old school textbook I'd seen once. It had been about punishments from the past – for thieves, murderers, or generally anyone who'd offended those in charge. They were publicly whipped, or put into stocks so people could throw rotten food at them. For the worst offenders, they were executed in front of large, jeering crowds.

This was the sight that met us as we returned home.

A crude wooden scaffold stood with three nooses hanging down, swaying gently in the wind.

A gaggle of Ys stood below, shouting, wailing, swearing. Standing on the platform were three Ys, clearly the ones in charge.

"They're getting ready to murder them," I breathed. "Their plan to takeover must have succeeded."

"But they haven't yet," Brown said, trying to reassure me. "And by the sounds of it, they know they're in danger. Look, they're on edge, they know their time is limited. They know they can't hurt anyone until they've been given the antidote. We can reason with them."

I feared that when they saw us, chaos would ensue.

I pulled Brown back, careful to keep us concealed.

"We can't just pitch up in the middle of this, that mob could turn and tear us apart in their panic. You go and talk to them – see if you can gauge what they're thinking, see if you can broker a deal. Our safety and the safety of Myla, in exchange for the antidotes. I'll head to the lab and get the vials, so as soon as they agree to the terms, we can start treating them."

"Okay," he answered, sounding dubious. "But I don't know how much luck I'll have persuading them to spare Myla."

"But you must try – even if she's banished from the city, I can't let them kill her."

"I'll do my best."

I gave him a quick hug and then slunk round the side of the building, heading to the lab.

*

613549. 613549. I typed the numbers in dutifully, certain I'd memorised the code from Ilana correctly. Both times the safe simply bleeped angrily and remained firmly closed.

Had I got it wrong? Had Ilana been mistaken?

I realised with dread that it was probably far more likely that Myla had again been one step ahead of us. It made sense that she would have changed the code to avoid a scenario like this. She'd have known Ilana would share it with me. We could only have a matter of hours to save the Ys from the fatal vaccine: I had to find where Myla was being kept and get her to give me the code.

The school building itself was deserted. The Ys were crowded outside, anxiously waiting for our return – I could only hope that Brown would be able to exert some authority over the ringleaders, with the promise of the antidote in exchange. I ran down corridors, checking in rooms as I passed. Instinctively, I headed to the Y quarters. As the area they knew best, this was most likely where they'd be keeping Myla and her followers.

The building got shabbier the further in I got, until I reached the end of the rabbit warren of corridors and swing doors. I was faced with what looked like maintenance cupboards, with faded lettering reading CLEANING CLOSET and CARETAKERS. I tried the handles of each. The first held mops and buckets, but not a lot else. The next one was locked.

I banged on the door. "Can anyone hear me?" I shouted. Muffled voices and sounds of movement.

I couldn't hear clearly; I put my ear to the door. "Hello? Myla, is that you?" I called again.

"You've found me, Sis!" I heard through the keyhole, her tone surprisingly upbeat despite her current predicament. She clearly still felt she had the upper-hand. "Now you need to head to my quarters – I keep a skeleton key in my bedside drawer. And I'd hurry if I were you – the clock's ticking for those miserable Ys".

In a final act of desperation, I shoved the door with my shoulder. It didn't budge. I turned and ran. I needed to get that key, get Myla out and then find Brown.

BROWN

TWENTY-FOUR

Heading towards the platform on which the gallows rested, the air felt thick with pain and fear. Everyone was looking to Eeyore for answers. Some were jeering, calling for Myla to be killed now. Others were desperately checking their bodies for signs of disease.

I shoved my way forward, briefly acknowledging Red and Orange, who barely registered my return. I headed determinedly for Eeyore. When he caught sight of me, he stretched out a hand and pulled me up onto the platform, giving me the height to clamber up beside him.

"The antidote – where is it?" Eeyore demanded, an unhinged look in his eyes. "Myla said her sister would come back and that she might have you with her. Did you betray us?" Eyes wide and hollow, he shook me by the shoulders.

"No! I was planning to run away, but I had nothing to do with this." Eeyore stared me down, before letting me go reluctantly, perhaps realising that until the effects of the vaccine had been reversed, he was pretty powerless.

"We came back to help stop her," I carried on. "Cara can get the antibodies, there's still time to reverse any ill effects."

"You're sure?" Hope dawned in his eyes, before something else closed that light down. "What's the catch?" he asked. "What's in it for you and her?" He spat the final word, betraying his feelings towards Cara as well as Myla.

I drew myself up tall. "You release Myla unharmed." Eeyore scoffed in disbelief, but I ploughed on regardless. "Cara and I walk free – we wanted to leave Galex anyway. You let us take Myla out from the city too. You guys get to stay here and be part of a new society."

"You and her going – I can live with that. But the Boss? I can't stop all of these guys from taking well-earned revenge."

"What choice do you have?" I asked reasonably. "It's our lives for yours."

Eeyore looked murderous, but he stayed quiet, accepting I was right.

I could only hope that once the antidotes were given, we'd have the chance to get away from them before they demanded vengeance. I didn't care what happened to Myla, but if Cara wanted her safe I would have to respect that.

CARA

TWENTY-FIVE

The lock clunked as the key turned. Once inside, I groped for the light switch, illuminating a small, dank cupboard. The occupants hid their eyes from the bright bulb – Orla, Mags and Myla, looking like moles emerging from a hole as they grew used to the light. All except Myla, whose dark eyes stared directly at me.

"You didn't think I'd leave anything to chance, did you, Sis?"

"I take it you mean the passcode," I replied, as I started to help them to their feet. I couldn't risk undoing the ropes knotted around their wrists yet – not when they outnumbered me three to one. I had to get them back out to Brown, so some sort of agreement could be reached. I could only hope the assembled mob would let us speak.

"The only place that passcode is now, is in my memory. If anything happens to me, those Ys are all dead."

"Strange as it may seem, I don't want anything bad to happen to you. But I also can't let the Ys die needlessly."

"Seems we're at a bit of an impasse then, Sis."

With everyone up, it was time to move.

"Myla, we'll have to come up with something. The alternative is we all die."

Myla swaggered forward. "Well, then. Let's see what deal we can reach."

We headed back down the corridor, with me leading the way, back to face the Ys.

*

As soon as the Ys laid eyes on us, the calls started: did we have the antidote? What was to happen to Myla?

Violence was there – at this stage muted, but I feared that as soon as Myla revealed the passcode, we'd lose control. Brown stood awkwardly with a gloomy-looking Y who seemed to be in control of the mutiny. Even from a distance, I could see his face was blanched with fear. He could feel it too – an atmosphere so charged that it spun on a knife edge.

Myla was the only one to look calm.

"Simmer down!" she bellowed, still a commanding presence, despite her weakened position. "You listen up and you'll get your cure. Loosen our restraints," she ordered, addressing me.

I hesitated, which angered her further. "Come on! You know we don't have weapons. These two are about as much use in a fight as a bunch of flowers, anyway," she muttered, gesturing towards Mags and Orla.

Weighing up my options, I loosened their hands, leaving Myla until last. A groan of protestation rose up around me as

I set my sister free. I stared at Brown, trying to communicate to him what was going on. He must have intuited a problem, because he yelled,

"Wait a minute! We need to listen to what Cara has to say. Remember we're here to help."

The crowd grumbled but a reluctant hush fell.

"I know you don't want to see Myla go free, but choices are limited," I spoke nervously, a sea of angry faces weighing my every word. "Our priority has to be getting the antidote to you. Before it's too late."

"Where is it then?" A belligerent voice called up from the crowd.

"Under my control," Myla spoke clearly and confidently, despite being so outnumbered. "I am the only person with access to it. And you've just kept me locked up for hours. Guess whether I'm keen to give it up?"

A fierce growl arose.

"Let's just tear her apart now!" a different voice shouted.

"She was never planning on letting us live, so let's just destroy her!"

Calls of agreement echoed across the courtyard, and for a moment it seemed we had lost control.

"Wait!" screamed the sad-eyed Y, stepping forward to grab Orla. "Give us the code or I'll kill her now!"

"Be my guest," Myla replied calmly. "But any X gets hurt and that's it for you lot."

We were deadlocked. I realised we would have to play up to Myla to get what we wanted – she was too stubborn to give in and, unlike everyone else, she had no problem with the Ys all dying.

"Okay, Myla," I said wearily. "What do we have to do in order for you to tell us the passcode?"

"That's more like it, Sis!" she said proudly. "I knew you'd come around. Well, if you're insistent that they must live, then all Ys are to be immediately banished from Galex. They're no longer welcome. That includes Lover Boy over there," she pointed her thumb towards Brown.

"Okay, fine," I agreed.

"You will stay in Galex with me."

"Agreed."

"I want this lead one dead." She pointed to the Y who had threaded Orla.

I hesitated. "We can sort that out as soon as we have the passcode."

Myla laughed. "Oh Sis, you're too easy to read. You could never fool me. You've no intention of doing any of those things, have you?"

"You know I'll do what I have to if it means you'll save their lives!"

She sighed, her laughter gone. "So you say now. But as soon as they've been cured, you'll leave me again. So why should I help them?"

I could feel myself giving up. She had the power – without that passcode, a lot of Ys were going to die. If she didn't trust me to stay with her, I'd have to tell her something she could believe.

"Myla, I can't stay here with you. Not after this. There'd always be something you'd want, or something you'd hold over me. I need the chance to be free and try and make a go of things with Brown and the baby. But you can be a part of that! You are my sister; you can still be a part of my life."

"And you think I'd be happy with that? Playing second best to a Y?"

"It's all I can offer you. Look, we came back. To help you, to help them. This situation can't carry on. I don't want you to do something you'll regret, but I can't lie to you. I can only appeal to the better nature that I know you have. If you love me at all, you'll give me the passcode before it's too late."

I searched her eyes for emotion, a link between us. In their darkness, I thought I could see a spark of something. I hoped it was her humanity.

I'd not been watching the Y stood with Brown, so intent was my focus on Myla. He'd edged closer to us and suddenly grabbed Myla, forcing her neck into one of the nooses and pulling her chin down. He had the strength of the insane: as he rammed her head down, her cheeks began to turn purple as she gasped pointlessly for air.

"Give me the code!" he shrieked, pausing briefly to let her up for air, before starting the assault again.

"Leave her! Let her speak!" I shouted, trying to loosen the rope from her neck by wedging my fingers between it and her skin. Myla's eyes bulged and began to empty.

The Y was roughly pulled back, and I turned to see Brown drag him away. Myla fell to her knees, gasping for breath. Her neck was ringed with deep bruising, turning a blackish tinge already.

"See, Sis? That's what you're saving," she croaked. A strange smile playing on her lips.

"Okay, you win. I'll give you the code. Then it can be a race to see who lives and who dies." She looked back at Orla and Mags. "Let's get ready to run, ladies. I've a feeling

we won't be welcome here when these Ys are all better."
Something passed between the expressions of the three Xs.

Still panting, Myla continued, "the code is 8 … 6 … 5 …"

"How many digits?" asked the lead Y wildly.

"6," I murmured, still unsure if Myla would give us the true code.

"2 … 2 … 9 … Now!"

With a quick look at Mags, Myla pointed to the Y who'd just tried to strangle her. Mags sprang on him, armed with what looked like a syringe filled with blue liquid. It found its home in his neck before anyone realised what was going on.

On the other side of the platform, Orla lunged towards 5 and 6, who'd joined Brown during the tumult.

"Go, Orla!" Myla instructed, as she watched her protégée plunge a needle into 5's leg. Realising I was still standing next to her, she gave me a good shove, causing me to stumble away from her, off the platform and onto the dirt below.

"Myla, what have you done?" I climbed back on my feet.

The two injected Ys looked sick with fear, before they began to scrabble at their skin. I'd seen this before, on a street long ago, when my mum was still around to rescue me.

A sly smile spread across Myla's face.

"I suggest you get your antidote pretty quickly if you're going to get out of here alive. We worked out how to do it – how to get them to mutate. In minutes, you'll be facing two Saurians."

MYLA

TWENTY-SIX

I need a distraction – what's better than creating two monsters before their very eyes? I know I've lost Cara, and this is my nuclear option. I can use this situation to get away, start again.

That doesn't mean I won't take my revenge first, though.

I walk towards him. Don't take my eyes from him. He doesn't see me, he's focused on what's happening to the other Y near him, who starts pawing at his face, as if he's been doused in acid. I raise the syringe, the needle an eye glinting in the light. Hold it up. I begin to run, slowly at first, but gathering pace. I see nothing but him. Gripping tight, I pull my arm back, sight trained on his neck, the vein I can see pulsing. His life blood. Wrist raised, down I plunge.

But wait … something heavy clunks my forearm. In a dream-like sequence, I see my hand sever from my wrist, and drop. Clattering to the ground next to my limb is an axe.

The syringe falls, shatters. Brown sees me now, realises what had been about to happen. His eyes stare at the syringe, oozing.

I stare at my wrist, oozing.

I look up, search around. What happened?

I see Cara. My sister.

She's leaning forward. It looks as if she's just thrown an axe directly at me.

CARA

TWENTY-SEVEN

"What have you done?"

Myla seemed genuinely shocked as she pieced together the last few seconds.

When I'd seen her move, with such determination, I knew that no matter what else was happening, I had to keep her in my sights. Her eyes never left Brown.

He was oblivious, as seemed everyone else. 5's transformation was beginning, and was turning out to be quite the showstopper.

It wasn't until she raised her arm that I realised what she was planning to do. The same blue venom that had just been the catalyst for 5's mutation looked azure in the sun.

Instinct took over. I'd no weapon, having been frisked when we arrived back in Galex. I scanned my immediate surroundings from my position beneath the platform. A Y, not far to my left. An axe in his hand. With no more thought, I'd moved to grab it, counting on him being distracted by the Saurian emerging before our eyes.

With the weapon in hand, I took aim. Where to hit her?
I'd had no more time to think.

Before I even realised it, I'd thrown the axe at my sister.

BROWN

TWENTY-EIGHT

If there's anything that'll distract you from a close brush with death, it's your friend turning into a full-grown Saurian in front of your eyes. I barely registered how close I'd come to the same fate, when 5's entire body began to quiver. I didn't even notice what happened to Myla in the seconds after she stood dumbly, staring at the bleeding stump where her hand had been only moments before. She seemed to regain her focus before I did though: by the time I'd looked back at her, after glancing again at 5, she'd disappeared, trailing blood like breadcrumbs.

There was no option but to jump down from the platform and back away from 5. The twitching motions became more and more erratic, and a screech escaped his lips. As I watched in horror, my friend disappeared – it looked like he had been swallowed. Now, in his place, a monster crouched. Slowly standing, it stretched long muscly legs, snarling viciously as it surveyed its surroundings. Clearly lost, its head went back, and it bellowed – an ear-piercing, deafening shriek. Mere metres away, stood another, even larger beast: Eeyore's transformation was also complete.

*

"Cara, I want you out of the way!" I yelled across to her, as she stared transfixed by the sight of the mutations. "Go and try the safe – check the passcode works."

She nodded and dashed off towards the building, keeping low so as not to attract the beasts' attention.

5 left no time in wreaking a path of destruction as he got used to his new body and strength. I reminded myself that this wasn't 5 anymore, and wouldn't be again. For now, though, there was no time to mourn the loss of a friend. If we didn't act quickly, the antidote would be pointless – we'd all be dead anyway.

5 snarled, smashing down on the nooses, ripping the gibbets from the platform to hurl them at the terrified Ys surrounding it. The crowd backed up quickly, but the courtyard was fairly enclosed, and no one seemed to want to be the first to openly run for it.

Someone took a risk and made for the gate to the left of 5. With the speed of a chameleon's tongue, the Saurian pounced. The crunching of bones punctuated the silence of shock as the rest of us could only watch in horror. Eeyore sniffed the air, seemingly drawn by the scent of blood. In seconds it'd joined 5 to feast on the Y, with cracking, chewing, ripping noises turning our stomachs.

"What the hell are we going to do?" asked 6, eyes wide as

he surveyed the two beasts getting to grips with their meal. "Any ideas?"

"Maybe. We need to separate them – both together, I think they'd be too strong." I was desperately trying to think about how I'd seen the recruits battle the Saurians, and the patterns they used to herd them where they wanted. "If we can get them apart, we might have a chance to at least contain them before the rest get back from the mission."

6 never took his eyes off the lizards. "Well, whatever you've got man, now's the time to share. Because in a few minutes they're going to be looking for their next course."

"You're right, I know. Do you think you could lead one of them away? Get it into the massive freezer down past the kitchen? If we can get it locked in, we can leave it trapped there for the recruits to deal with."

6 appraised the plan, then nodded thoughtfully. "That's not a bad idea. D'you think you can handle the other one?"

"I can try." I had an idea that, if everything went to plan, might just work.

*

"Listen up!" I addressed the 30 or so Ys in the courtyard, some paralysed with fear, others edging as far from the Saurians as they could. With the beasts blocking the exit out, the only option was to go through the school. The thought of being trapped inside by one of the lizards obviously didn't appeal, as no one had yet moved too far towards the heavy swing door.

"We need to act quickly if we're going to avoid the same fate." I pointed to the remains of the body the Saurians were still munching on and noticed from the corner of my eye that Eeyore was already showing interest in the Y nearest to him.

"People on my right," I gestured with my arm, "I need you to help 6 lure Eeyore into the deep freeze. It's big enough to hold him and the cold should put him into a diapause state, slowing him down. He'll be contained in there until the real soldiers get back."

The Ys looked scared, but they nodded in agreement. "The two closest to the school doors: in a minute I need you to run as fast as you can and get the freezer doors open. The rest of you need to try and aggravate Eeyore – throw rocks, missiles, anything you can think of. We need it to chase 6 to the freezer and once it's in, the door needs shutting."

I let this sink in. It was a plan filled with holes. Would Eeyore take the bait? Would 6 outrun it? How would he get it into the freezer without being trapped himself? How many Ys would it take to shut a door against the strength of a Saurian? I couldn't answer any of these questions for definite – I could only hope that, with a bit of luck, the idea would work.

"Jeez, could you have come up with anything riskier?" 6 sounded exasperated. "Not loving my role in the plan, either," he muttered, hand on the back of his head.

"It's all I've got, dude," I said. "You up for it?"

A sudden movement. Eeyore swooped onto another Y, claws ripping out his throat and silencing his scream in a second.

"Doesn't look like there's much choice. Anything's better than standing here waiting to be next in line at the lizard buffet."

"I take it we're all on board?" Horrified nods as the second of our group was consumed before our eyes.

"What you got in mind for the Saurian formerly known as 5?" 6 asked.

"Something more destructive. Orange and Red," I called to my friends, who'd been sidling as close to the wall as possible. "Red, I need the petrol for the mower. And matches or lighters, whatever you can find. Orange, can you find me glass bottles and a few cloths? Be as fast as you can and then meet me in the garden round the back of our quarters. The rest of you –" my eyes searched out the remaining 15 or so Ys, "you need to help me get 5 there."

CARA

TWENTY-NINE

I knew Brown was right: this was a fight I couldn't lead. The passcode became a chant running through my head so I wouldn't forget it, as I pushed my way in through the swing door and down the corridor heading to the science labs.

She must have guessed this was where I'd head. I was opening the door to the main laboratory when I felt it.

An arm round my neck. "Don't struggle," a voice rasped. Delilah held me tight, her red frizz tickling my cheek. The icy steel of a knife kissed my throat. Where she'd come from I had no idea – I could only imagine the Ys had locked her up separately to my sister, but she'd escaped or been set free.

Myla.

My sister was in front of me. I took in her appearance: the pale face, drained of blood and warmth. The arm, a tourniquet stemming the blood loss from her wrist. Her other shoulder slumped over Delilah, who seemed to be supporting her weight. Her eyes were what stopped me cold, though. Two black pits stared emptily at me.

She held up her stump. "You did this," she hissed, her eyes onyx and cold. "To save a Y? After everything I've done for you?"

"I'm sorry, you left me no choice." He's the father of my child, I left unsaid.

"You will always have a choice. You chose them. I choose Xs. And I choose to honour Mum."

I shook my head, understanding clearly for perhaps the first time that Myla was too damaged for me to bring back from the brink this time. Nothing would alter her course of destruction against the Ys, not even her need to protect me. And now I'd broken her trust by saving Brown at her expense.

"I vowed to protect you, to look after you. And this is how you repay me?"

I looked at her arm. The blood was flowing less quickly, but she was still losing a fair amount. For the first time, I noticed the knife in her other hand. A gripe of fear rippled across my body. My hand reflexively covered my stomach, a gesture not lost on Myla.

"Ah yes," she purred, stepping closer, the tip of the blade coming closer, until it pressed against my skin. "One slice and I could open you up right here, watch you bleed out." Her black eyes bored into mine. The sharp edge of the knife pierced my belly. I flinched, before closing my eyes and steeling myself for the worst.

"Please, no," I begged, opening my eyes again, searching for any remnants of humanity in hers.

"Don't worry, Sis," she whispered, mouth so close to my ear I could feel the wetness of her lips. "That would be too easy. Best let this little one grow and get bigger. It'll hurt you more when I take it then."

In a final gesture of power, she grabbed my cheeks and kissed my lips, a final perverse goodbye.

The knife was removed from my throat, I was shoved to the ground, and my sister was gone.

*

With the taste of Myla's mouth on mine, I had no time to process her threats, or even mourn the fact that this sealed the end of our relationship. If the Ys were to survive, I had to find the antibodies. The safe was in the cupboard in the far corner of the main lab – I headed straight to it and punched in the code. I could only hope that Myla had given the correct numbers and that this wasn't a final act of vengeance against the Ys. My breath exhaled as the safe swung open and I lifted out the vials of antibodies. I set to work transferring the liquid into syringes, ready to inject.

BROWN

THIRTY

"NOW!"

There was no perfect time to do it. In the end, we just had to put both feet in and jump. On my shout, the two Ys selected legged it into the school. The remaining gaggle started pelting Eeyore with any debris to hand: some had crude weapons to throw, others just grabbed bits of wood from the platform or stones from the courtyard.

For a minute, I thought it was never going to work. Eeyore barely noticed it was being assaulted. It licked its lips slowly, savouring the last bit of flesh. It wasn't until 6 clonked it on the head with a statue of a half-naked lady from the old fountain, that it began to realise it was under attack.

"Come on, then!" yelled 6, sounding far more confident than I felt. The beast exhaled through its nose, saliva spraying outwards. 6 turned and ran straight into the school building.

"Surround it from behind!" I shouted, hoping desperately that the lizard would follow 6. After a brief pause, it darted forwards and stormed inside, pulling the door from its hinges in rage.

"Chase it! You've got to get it locked in!" I yelled again, watching the Saurian charge with growing speed. The remaining Ys sped after it.

Please let this work, I thought.

*

"What are we going to do with this one?" Red panted, his face the colour of his name as he handed me the jerry cans, petrol spilling over. Digging in his pocket, he passed over a couple of lighters too. "I grabbed a handful of these."

"We need to get it into a contained space. If we can push it through the gate into the old kitchen garden, we should be able to hold it there. I can't risk it getting inside the building." Not when that's where Cara is, I added mentally.

"Orange, did you get those things?"

"Yup." He passed me three glass bottles and a pile of dish rags. In return, I gave him a lighter.

I set to work filling the bottles half full with the petrol and stoppering the mouth of each bottle with a rolled-up cloth. Tipping the bottles up, I made sure the bottoms of the rags were soaked in the pungent liquid, before handing one to each of my friends.

"When I say so, you're going to need to light the top of the cloth and then throw these as hard as you can – keep them upright for now."

The remaining Saurian was starting to look restless. It began swiping wildly at any nearby Ys, catching a couple with blows strong enough to knock them out. We needed to move quickly if we were going to have enough conscious bodies.

"Grab anything you can that will help you keep it at a distance!" I shouted, keeping Orange and Red back, well out of the path of the flailing beast. "Wood from the platform, branches. We need to form an arrow shape and funnel the thing through the gate!"

The Ys galvanised. Armed, they advanced, a couple of large hunters at the front, risking the swinging claws. Angered, 5 tried to grab at the weapons, hurling some at other Ys. One fell, not moving. There wasn't time to stop, though – the longer 5 was loose like this, the more people it would kill. Slowly, the bravest at the front of the arrow shape started jabbing at the Saurian with large wooden poles, once part of the gibbet intended for Myla, and the group managed to force it back to the gate, towards the kitchen garden.

"Keep going! You're nearly there!" I encouraged. There was still another element to the plan that needed putting in place.

"Bugs!" I called. A small, skinny Y with buck teeth and a squint looked up from the back of the group. I gestured to him.

"You still a good climber?" He nodded, displaying his large front teeth in pride. "I need you to take this jerry can and carry it up onto the roof, over the Y dormitories. Stay at the edge until I yell – then I need you to hurl it as hard as you can at the Saurian's head."

Bugs nodded again and took the can, petrol slopping in large droplets onto the ground. He turned and ran, quick and nimble.

5 roared again, and grabbed one of the wooden poles from the hands of the largest hunter. It smashed the post repeatedly on the ground in front of it, causing the Ys to stagger back, with some scattering in fear.

"Just a bit further!" I yelled again, desperate for the good work already done not to go to waste.

"Let's do this!" picked up the largest hunter. Leading the way with a roar himself, the group surged forwards. 5 turned and walked into the garden carrying the stick and swinging it like a golf club. Two more Ys were knocked from their feet, but this time the Saurian was through the gate and into the garden. I searched the roof, before catching sight of Bugs dropping onto his knees on the ledge, giving me the thumbs up.

It was now or never.

*

"Throw it, Bugs!" The Y on the roof stood, jerry can lifted high. He launched it at 5. Sailing through the air, it went unnoticed by the Saurian until it clunked it on the head. Roaring in rage, it grabbed up the can and locked its jaws around it, piercing the metal. Petrol dripped down its mouth and body.

"Get back!" I shouted to the remaining Ys, watching them retreat pretty sharpish. "Red and Orange, now it's your turn." I took my lighter and held it to the rag stuffed in my milk bottle, the other two copying my example. When it had caught, I let the flame take hold, before hurling it towards 5. It smashed at its feet, a fireball engulfing the plants to its left.

5 howled, before two more petrol bombs followed mine. The first was wide to the right, the explosion missing the Saurian completely. The second was a direct hit, shattering as it met 5's torso. Mixing with the petrol already dousing its body, the lizard was consumed with flames. It shrieked in agony, trying to escape the heat and fire, which melted its scaly skin. The heat coming off it was intense. Shielding our eyes, we backed up to behind the gate, pulling it shut. The beast ran towards us in a final panic, before smacking against the gate's metal bars. It stayed there, roasting, still moaning in pain.

"That is sick, man," Red spoke finally, unable to take his eyes off the creature. "I'd almost feel sorry for the thing, if it hadn't just eaten several of my friends right in front of me."

"And the stench," Orange added. He wasn't wrong; the reek of burnt flesh was pretty overpowering.

Despite the relief we all felt at having defeated a dangerous foe, Red was right: it felt like a hollow victory. 5 had been a Y just like us. It felt wrong to celebrate the death of the Saurian. I felt anger surge in my chest: this was down to Myla.

I turned away from the sight of the burning body, searching the courtyard. 6 loped up, his cheerful face telling me his mission had also been successful.

"We did it, man!" he crowed. "One hot lizard and one cold. I was lucky the thing was running so fast: when I stopped and dodged at the last minute, it just kept on flying into the freezer. The door's holding tight, but I've left a group of Ys guarding it anyway. With any luck, by the time the Xs get back, it'll be having a kip in the corner, trying to keep warm."

"That's fantastic, well done, mate," I said, clapping him on the back.

My eyes kept searching, until I found her.

In a corner by the school entrance, the Ys were already lining up, waiting for their injection. At least it seemed Myla had given us the correct passcode – perhaps it had all been part of a big game to her, to watch us scrabble around and see if we managed to get the antidote in time. Whatever her motive, I suspected she was long gone, at least for the time being. Seeing Cara in one piece and finally free of her gave me back that feeling of lightness: our future together was still possible.

The atmosphere in the courtyard was one of exhilaration. Ys rejoiced over our victory, tended to the wounded and waited for their injections. I was met with a lot of hugs, whoops and admiration, which I shrugged off, keen to reach Cara.

By the time I got over to her though, something was happening. I was met with the sight of her on the floor, face grimacing in pain. She was clasping her hand to her stomach, doubled over in agony.

She spoke two words.

"The baby."

SIX MONTHS LATER

EPILOGUE

BROWN

Slipping a hand underneath the little bundle in front of me, I cautiously lifted her. Our baby. I still couldn't believe that we'd created such a perfect being. Her tiny rosebud mouth, her scrunched up face. The softest skin I'd ever felt. A warmth flooded me every time I looked into her face. I felt a sense of belonging and peace that I'd never before experienced.

When I'd seen Cara clutch her stomach in pain after the defeat of the Saurians, I'd feared the worst. She'd been through so much trauma, it wouldn't have been much of a surprise if she'd suffered a miscarriage. All I could do was lift her up and carry her to the infirmary and keep her still until Ilana got back.

The recruits dealt fairly easily with the refrigerated Saurian: the cold had caused it to shut down to preserve fat and energy. It was very groggy and so not too hard to put an end to.

Things were touch and go with Cara for a few weeks. We could only hope that plenty of rest and a stress-free time would help her carry the baby to full term.

Blocking out stress was easier said than done. With the Saurians dead and the Ys saved, we could relax a bit, but Myla was still AWOL. And not only her: Delilah, Mags and Orla were all with her, with Mimi and Chantelle still unaccounted for too. And, by the looks of it, a stash of the venom needed for mutations. From her last threat to Cara, it sounded like she was prepared to wait to get back at her sister, but there was no guarantee she wouldn't change her mind and be back to wreak havoc anytime she wanted.

Galex had transformed too. The actions of Myla and her subsequent vanishing act, and the defeat of the Saurians by the Ys, had given the city an air of hope. Real change seemed possible.

The Xs were still wary – and I couldn't completely blame them. There was still no vaccine, therefore no guarantee that mutations wouldn't naturally occur. The injections of X antibodies became regular though – the hope being that even if the Epidemic returned, Ys would have at least some protection from its effects. Ilana had got to work again on a new vaccine, revitalised by the more pressing need to reverse the effects of the blue venom Myla had managed to harness. I didn't doubt that she'd crack it in the end.

For now, there was a cautious unity. Everyone was in it together, with Xs helping Ys rather than fearing them.

The hope is that a vaccine would be named after our daughter – a symbol of an X and Y union.

CARA

Xyla. The perfect name for the perfect baby. A gesture that's meant to say, there's a different future for the Ys. From something damaged can grow something beautiful. I look at her still, and my heart could burst with love. I'm so grateful that Brown and I both survived to meet her and can't wait to get to know her better as she grows up.

It won't be here, though – at least not yet. I can't stay here anymore than Brown can. For him, the ghosts are slavery, pain and sacrifice. For me, the only ghost is Myla, but she haunts me wherever I go. Her final words to me, the threat to take my child – they echo down every street of the city. I hear them in my nightmares. Although I've no proof and we've seen no trace of her since she disappeared, I'm convinced she's still alive. If nothing else, she's a survivor. I have no doubt that she'll come for me one day. For us. I wasn't about to make it easier for her by staying put in the city she knew best.

*

In the few months after the mutations and Myla's escape, everyone worked together as a unit to rebuild.

Instead of a dictatorship, the city has become more of a democracy. For the first time in a long time, the future feels bright, no matter what your genetic make-up.

The Saurians are still out there, and the worry is they may keep evolving. However, after the recent mission's triumph, there's a lot more confidence about how to defeat even a large group of them. The success of using vaccinated Y blood to poison them can be replicated and plans to attack other nests are already underway. Callie's already taken on my role as City Protector and is planning to lead the recruits out again soon. I know I'm leaving the city safe in her hands.

For us though, a new challenge. Amex. Brown has this idea it'll be like a wonderland, he's so excited to get there. He tries to hide it, wants me to be happy, but I know how desperate he is to reach the city. I wonder if he feels like he owes it to the friends he's lost.

Not that I blame him. He's been through so much and sacrificed such a lot. I might feel less certain about the place, but I won't show him that. I'm going there for him. And for Xyla. They're more important than Galex, or Myla: they are my family now.

"All set?" Ilana had appeared in the doorway. She surveyed my room: the tiny crib, the meagre baggage. We were taking as little as we could – although with a baby, it felt like we were carrying half the world on our backs. Brown had a romantic idea of a complete fresh start; said we didn't need any possessions. He hadn't factored in the demands of keeping a 12-week-old baby fed, clean and entertained though.

"I think so," I answered, taking a final look at my dorm before shouldering my bag, shifting Xyla to my other hip. We were being accompanied at least part of the way by a couple of recruits, in case Myla was lying in wait just outside the walls.

"Here, let me. Hi baby," she cooed. "Say goodbye to Auntie Ilana." She planted a big wet kiss on Xyla's cheek, making her squeal with delight.

"I'll miss you both so much!" she said, tears in her eyes.

"We'll miss you too," I replied, hugging her awkwardly under my bag. "It won't be forever though, I'm sure. We need to be less isolated, bring surviving communities together. This is the first step to creating better paths and communications between the cities." "True," Ilana sighed. "I just hope it doesn't take too long."

"Me too," I answered honestly, realising just how much I'd miss my best friend.

*

"You ready?" Brown asked, smoothing his golden hair self-consciously. He was still getting used to it and was already insanely proud of his growing mane.

"As I'll ever be," I answered smiling.

"You sure about this?" His eyes were worried.

"I am." Looking at Xyla, I was certain. She needed to grow up in a world where both her parents were seen as equals. She needed to not be living under the shadows that hung over Galex for both of us. I owed it to her to give her that. With her and Brown, I had everything I would need.

There was only a small group to see us off – we hadn't wanted a lot of fuss. Most of our goodbyes had already been said. And, as we liked to say, it was only a goodbye for now: we'd be back, I was sure of it. Maybe with a vaccine, maybe with new friends, but we'd see this city again. I wanted to see what it could become, with Ilana at the helm. It was always meant to be a beacon, a place of hope. It had just lost its way on the journey.

I took Brown's hand in mine, shifting Xyla onto my left side. "It's time," I said. "We're a family now," I added simply.

Brown cupped my face in his hand, kissed me and then our daughter.

"She looks just like you," he smiled at me. "She's even got the same determined mouth."

Except for one thing.

"She has your eyes," I said.

Together, we stepped out of the gates.